Dear Reader,

Happy New Year from Silhouette Desire, where we offer you six passionate, powerful and provocative romances every month of the year! Here's what you can indulge yourself with this January....

Begin the new year with a seductive MAN OF THE MONTH, *Tall, Dark & Western* by Anne Marie Winston. A rancher seeking a marriage of convenience places a personals ad for a wife, only to fall—hard—for the single mom who responds!

Silhouette Desire proudly presents a sequel to the wildly successful in-line continuity series THE TEXAS CATTLEMAN'S CLUB. This exciting *new* series about alpha men on a mission is called TEXAS CATTLEMAN'S CLUB: LONE STAR JEWELS. Jennifer Greene's launch book, *Millionaire M.D.*, features a wealthy surgeon who helps out his childhood crush when she finds a baby on her doorstep—by marrying her!

Alexandra Sellers continues her exotic miniseries SONS OF THE DESERT with one more irresistible sheikh in *Sheikh's Woman.* THE BARONS OF TEXAS miniseries by Fayrene Preston returns with another feisty Baron heroine in *The Barons of Texas: Kit.* In Kathryn Jensen's *The Earl's Secret,* a British aristocrat romances a U.S. commoner while wrestling with a secret. And Shirley Rogers offers *A Cowboy, a Bride & a Wedding Vow,* in which a cowboy discovers his secret child.

So ring in the new year with lots of cheer and plenty of red-hot romance, by reading all six of these enticing love stories.

Enjoy!

Joan Marlow Golan

Joan Marlow Golan
Senior Editor, Silhouette Desire

Please address questions and book requests to:
Silhouette Reader Service
U.S.: 3010 Walden Ave., P.O. Box 1325, Buffalo, NY 14269
Canadian: P.O. Box 609, Fort Erie, Ont. L2A 5X3

Millionaire M.D.

JENNIFER GREENE

Published by Silhouette Books

America's Publisher of Contemporary Romance

Special thanks and acknowledgment are given to
Jennifer Greene for her contribution to the
Texas Cattleman's Club: Lone Star Jewels series.

To my fellow Texas Cattleman's Club authors, Sara Orwig,
Cindy Gerard, Kristi Gold, Sheri WhiteFeather—
you were all so wonderful to work with! I hope we have another
chance to commit murder, mayhem and jewel thefts together.

 SILHOUETTE BOOKS

ISBN 0-373-76340-9

MILLIONAIRE M.D.

Visit Silhouette at www.eHarlequin.com

Printed in U.S.A.

Books by Jennifer Greene

Silhouette Desire

Body and Soul #263
Foolish Pleasure #293
Madam's Room #326
Dear Reader #350
Minx #366
Lady Be Good #385
Love Potion #421
The Castle Keep #439
Lady of the Island #463
Night of the Hunter #481
Dancing in the Dark #498
Heat Wave #553
Slow Dance #600
Night Light #619
Falconer #671
Just Like Old Times #728
It Had To Be You #756
Quicksand #786
*Bewitched #847
*Bothered #855
*Bewildered #861
A Groom for Red Riding Hood #893
Single Dad #931
Arizona Heat #966
†*The Unwilling Bride* #998
†*Bachelor Mom* #1046
Nobody's Princess #1087
A Baby in His In-Box #1129
Her Holiday Secret #1178
The Honor Bound Groom #1190
***Prince Charming's Child* #1225
***Kiss Your Prince Charming* #1245
Rock Solid #1316
Millionaire M.D. #1340

Silhouette Intimate Moments

Secrets #221
Devil's Night #305
Broken Blossom #345
Pink Topaz #418

Silhouette Special Edition

†*The 200% Wife* #1111

Silhouette Books

Birds, Bees and Babies 1990
"Riley's Baby"

Santa's Little Helpers 1995
"Twelfth Night"

Fortune's Children
The Baby Chase

Montana Mavericks
You Belong To Me

*Jock's Boys
†The Stanford Sisters
**Happily Ever After

JENNIFER GREENE

lives near Lake Michigan with her husband and two children. Before writing full-time, she worked as a teacher and a personnel manager. Michigan State University honored her as an "outstanding woman graduate" for her work with women on campus.

Ms. Greene has written more than fifty category romances, for which she has won numerous awards, including three RITAs from the Romance Writers of America in the Best Short Contemporary Books category, and a Career Achievement award from *Romantic Times Magazine*.

"What's Happening in Royal?"

NEWS FLASH, January—Royal, Texas, is in a state of shock! The plane that made an emergency crash landing in the nearby West Texas desert was carrying both a European contingent and some of Royal's own....

Just a few nights ago, all were reveling in the "Party of the Year" at the Texas Cattleman's Club to honor peace brought forth between archenemy European countries Obersbourg and Asterland...a feat our Texas Cattleman's Club members *may* have had a hand in. And to go from celebration to misery so quickly...can our boys come to the rescue once more?

Also, there's been a sighting of Winona Raye doing her cop thing—with a baby in tow! Sources tell us the tiny tot appeared on Winona's doorstep. Hmmm...perhaps dashing Dr. Justin Webb—card-carrying Texas Cattleman's Club member—will help out his childhood friend!

Stay tuned....

One

Ask Dr. Justin Webb, and "The Tennessee Waltz" was a downright ridiculous—if not insulting—song to play at a Texas bash, but what the hey. He didn't care what it took to get his arms around Winona. Never had. Never would. He didn't even mind having to wear a tux and be on his best starched behavior for an exhaustingly long evening, as long as he could catch some private moments with her now and then. Like this one.

"I swear, honey, you look good enough to marry."

"Why, thank you, doc." Wearing spindly tall dress pumps, Winona almost reached his cheek in height, but she still had to tilt her face to make eye contact. He marveled. Those eyes of hers were the same soft, wistful, breathtaking blue of a dawn sky—but her smile, so typically, was full of the devil. And that was when she was being reasonably nice to him. "You haven't proposed marriage to me in, what, two weeks now?"

Twelve days and six hours, but who was counting. "Give or take a few days."

She nodded demurely. "And how many times do I have to tell you? If I'm ever in the mood to marry a hard-core womanizing bachelor with way too much money, I'll let you know."

Justin grinned, since there was no point in taking the insult to heart. In the past, she'd dished out far, far worse.

Come to think of it, so had he.

Tightening his grip, he whirled her past the banquet table, the fiddlers, the receiving line of dignitaries and Asterland royalty. He wanted to waltz her past and out the tall balcony doors and into the star-studded night—where he'd have Win to himself—but the idea just wouldn't fly. Unfortunately, the January night was typical of west Texas, the temperature colder than a witch's heart, and the wind twice as bitter. "Well, shoot, darlin'. If I can't talk you into marriage tonight, how about a nice, immoral, amoral, down-and-dirty affair?"

"I'd love to, doc—with anyone else. But you've already done that with so many women in town that I'd just be one in a long line. Thanks, but no thanks."

He winced—not from her comment, but because she'd just stepped on his foot. God knew, Winona was adorable, but she *did* have the grace of a coyote on a dance floor. A hand at the small of her back coaxed her physically closer to him. Close enough for him to feel the tips of her nipples beneath the monk-black dress that zipped straight and plain, right to her throat. Close enough so that he could see her light blue eyes dilate when her tummy rubbed against his satin tux cummerbund. Close enough to see the spare, soft gloss on her small mouth.

Close enough to see her scowl.

"Behave yourself, you dog."

His eyebrows arched, trying out the charmingly innocent expression that had always worked on the softer sex. With one exception. "Now, Win, you know I'm just trying to help. I'm afraid you're going to trip and fall. And I know you're not fond of advice, but if you'd just quit trying to lead, I swear you'd have a lot easier time on the dance floor."

"You're trying to help? Said the wolf in the fox den. And *what* do you think your hand is doing on my butt? You think I won't punch you?"

Actually, he *knew* she'd punch him—in public, in private, in church, at a black-tie gala or anywhere else. She'd been doing it ever since she was a furious, bad-tempered twelve-year-old, and he'd been a suave, worldly seventeen who'd known everything—except why the hell such a squirt-age girl had managed to wind his heart around her finger. "I've had my hand on your butt before," he reminded her delicately.

"That was significantly different. I was hurt, I'd fallen on some broken glass and you were playing doctor—"

"And I'm so glad you brought that up. I never had a chance to tell you before how much I always loved playing doctor with you," he said fervently.

There now. She had to choke back laughter. Winona never could keep that terrific sense of humor under wraps for long—but this time, she turned serious again all too quickly. "Cut it out, you. And this time, I mean it. The point is, you know I'd never be attending this fancy shindig if I weren't working. Just because I'm not in a cop's uniform doesn't mean that I'm really here to play. I'm here in a professional role—which means that you either put your hand where it belongs, or I really just might slug you—and I'm not kidding, Justin."

He heard her. And he not only believed her, but he'd never have done anything to publicly embarrass her in a million years. A teasing pat was one thing, an inappropriate grope in front of others, another—not just because he respected Winona and her job, but because if he ever got a shot at really getting to Win, he wanted no audience around. Anywhere. Preferably for a several-hundred-mile radius.

Temporarily, however, it seemed that he was incapable of removing his hand from her fanny. It wasn't a choice. Normal honorable, ethical standards of behavior simply couldn't apply. His palm slid down the silky dress from the hollow of her spine to the fullest slope of her rump. He squeezed several times, because hell, he had to.

Said squeezing produced the obvious biological response in him—he was hard as a hammer in three seconds flat. Above the neck, though, his forehead produced a frown darker than a Texas thunderstorm. "What in God's name are you wearing under that dress?"

He would never have asked the question, except that the answer seemed to be nothing. Absolutely nothing. There wasn't a woman in the Club—except for Winona—who wasn't dripping diamonds and sequins. Jewels winked from ears, throats, wrists and fingers, all across the dance floor. Win's ears were naked and so was her throat; the long, soft black dress made all the pricey designer gowns look overdone and fussy. To Justin, she stood out as a hopeless beauty. Always had, in his eyes.

It was just…he couldn't feel any underwear. He certainly hadn't put his hand on her fanny *expecting* to feel underwear. But the silky dress was a thinnish material, so that his hand instinctively expected to find panty lines, a sense of fabric. And when they didn't, alarm bells clanged in his mind on a par with a fire truck's siren. There weren't too many reasons a woman would neglect to wear underwear to a very public, very fancy gig—especially Winona, who didn't reveal nuttin' to no one—normally. When it came down to it, Justin could only think of one reason she'd be running around sans panties. There had to be a lover she was trying to turn on.

A lover.

A man.

A man—who wasn't him.

"Justin, what the Sam Hill is the matter with y—"

He sensed her right fist clenching, preparing to punch him.

"Get your hand off my... The dress showed lines," she hissed. "I couldn't wear anything underneath it. Not that I owe you any explanation, you low-down, overprotective, bossy son of a gun. Now you've got five seconds, max, before I—"

He was removing his hand. Really. Right then. It just took a couple seconds for relief to catch up with him, and for those few seconds he really couldn't seem to breathe. In the meantime—possibly because Win didn't realize he was sincerely getting around to behaving better—that small right fist of hers was still aiming straight for his solar plexus. That is, until a tall, handsome, dark-haired dude showed up on the scene, winked at Win, and smoothly lifted her clenched fist to his right shoulder.

"I'm cutting in," Aaron Black announced, "before either of you come to blows. Besides which, I dance a ton better than he ever will, Winona. *And* I'm better looking."

"Well, hell," Justin grumbled. But he let Aaron take off with Winona across the dance floor. For one thing, the orchestra changed tunes to a rousing, foot-stomping bluegrass, so any cheek-to-cheek opportunities had abruptly disappeared. For another, Aaron was not only a fellow member of the Texas Cattleman's Club, but a friend that Justin would trust to the wall—and had. And for yet another reason, damn Aaron, but he was a diplomat in his professional life as well as his private one, and when he motioned a thumb toward the bar, Justin picked up the subtle, tactful clue that, just possibly, he needed to get out of Winona's sight for a minute or two.

He loped over to the bar, all right...but watching Win whirl off in Aaron's arms still gave him a case of the glums that a whole well of whiskey couldn't cure.

They'd always bickered like two toddlers in the same sandbox. Justin didn't specifically mind that, because they mutually enjoyed teasing each other. But she'd always treated him like a friend, a neighbor, a loved but insufferable big brother. Never as a man.

He must have asked her to marry him fifty times—and all fifty times, she'd cracked up laughing, as if the idea of marrying him was the best joke they'd ever shared.

He got it, he got it. It didn't matter if half the women in town chased him nonstop. Winona just couldn't seem to imagine him as a lover. For several years now, Justin kept thinking if she could just *need* him. If he could just get a chance to show her a different side of himself. If something could jolt her into looking at him differently, maybe, just maybe, he'd have a serious shot with her.

"Hi, Dr. Webb." Riley Monroe, the Club's longtime caretaker, had a smile waiting even before Justin reached the bar. "You guys sure outdid yourself with the party tonight. This is quite a shindig. What can I get you?"

"Whiskey. Straight. And thanks, Riley." Justin didn't have to wait thirty seconds before the glass of liquid gold was in his hands. Riley might be the Texas Cattleman's Club night caretaker, but he'd subbed as a bartender for formal functions for as long as Justin could remember. The ladies loved him—likely because he had a dose of flimflam in his character. Occasionally he could spread on the Las Vegas-type charm too thickly for Justin's taste, but that didn't matter. Riley was as dependable as the sunshine and as loyal as a hound. Good qualities in any man, and normally Justin would have chatted for a few minutes.

Tonight, he gulped down a big enough sip to feel the whiskey burn some new holes in his tonsils, then leaned back against the bar.

He spotted her, still out there, still high-stepping with Aaron…and damnation, looking like she was having a hell of a good time.

He looked around, determined to get his mind off Winona—and to keep it off. The party was in full swing, and although good taste had to be an issue with so many royal guests, so was having fun Texas-style. Messy, finger-dripping lobster and Texas barbecue was set up on the same table as the fragile hothouse roses and elegant ice sculptures. The formal orchestra was all dressed in black tie—but naturally, it had a damn good fiddling section. The giant boar's head hanging on one wall looked down on more diamonds and rubies than the bugger had ever seen in the wild, for darn sure, but the blaze of firelight winked on the iron-studded plaque over the entrance door. Leadership, Justice and Peace was burned into the wood—the long-term logo for the Club that had a uniquely special meaning this night.

Justin gulped down another slug of whiskey, trying to ignore the short-haired brunette dancing past him yet again. He winked at a blonde instead. The Princess Anna von Oberland of Obersbourg—at least that'd been her title until she'd married Greg, who was plastered against her on the dance floor in total oblivion to the foot-stomping, sassy rhythm of the current song being played.

The whole purpose of this black-tie shindig was Anna. An outsider would surely find the situation confounding—what could a bunch of Texans possibly have in common with royalty from the small European countries of Obersbourg and Asterland? But months earlier, Princess Anna had been in grave trouble, and the Texas Cattleman's Club had stepped in to rescue her. Two days from now, twelve citizens from both Asterland and Obersbourg were returning to Europe via private jet—without Anna, of course, who was head over heels for her bridegroom and Texas both. But this party was it. A chance for Anna's family—and government—to say thank you to the Texas Cattleman's Club boys…and a chance for the Club to strengthen the ties between the governments.

Justin finished the last gulp of whiskey, thinking how unusual this whole shindig was. Not the party itself. Truth to tell, the Texas Cattleman's Club used any excuse to throw a formal brawl—and the bigger the better. But the group generally kept a low profile about their "quieter" activities. The world was pretty damn lousy at protecting its innocents. It's not like the Club stuck its nose in a hornet's nest if there was any choice, but sometimes an innocent's life could hang in the balance—a situation where diplomacy either failed or where politics were so ticklish that tuning to normal channels simply didn't get results.

An edgy thought needled through Justin's mind, stealing the jubilant party mood and making him shift uneasily on his feet. He was the only Club member who didn't own a gun. He used to. His grandparents were big in ranching and oil both, and anyone owning a big spread who lived in that kind of isolated country knew how to handle a gun. So did Justin, but that was years ago. At this point, he was starkly aware that he was the only member who never shot anything but a hypodermic. The others had strong military skills in their background. He did his rescuing with a scalpel.

And there was nothing precisely wrong with that, but suddenly his mind was whirling, spinning down dark roads. He'd come home from Bosnia to abruptly and completely change medical specialties. No one had asked him why he'd switched to plastic surgery. No one had noticed that there were certain medical cases he no longer touched. And so far it hadn't mattered, because none of his private work with the Texas Cattlemen's Club had forced him into situations that he couldn't handle. But it could, Justin knew, and he feared letting his Club members down.

So far, thank God, the only one he'd let down was himself.

The orchestra suddenly changed to a slow dance. Swiftly, Justin lifted his head. A redhead winked at him as she sashayed past. Moments later, an elegant blonde wagged him a hello over her dance partner's shoulder.

He winked back and smiled back, but his heart wasn't in it. Tarnation, where had Winona disappeared to? Invariably he got a lot of female attention at these gigs, and that was nice, real nice, but primarily the reason he got such a rush from the single females in town was because of his wealthy, jet-set reputation.

The wealth was real enough—his grandparents had left him a ton, on top of what he hauled in as a plastic surgeon. But believe the social columns, and he only did tummy tucks and nose jobs when he wasn't taking off on impulsive, lavish vacations.

He not only didn't mind the stupid image. He catered to it. Since people expected him to disappear on a whim, it made his projects and missions with the Texas Cattleman's Club easier to pull off. In this particular situation, though, the media had been led to believe that some good old Texas boys had "accidentally" become involved in Princess Anna's dilemma. Justin had never kept his association with the Club a secret. He never kept secrets. Nothing in life got out faster or caused more trouble than a secret. But he *did* believe in keeping quiet when….

There she was. Win. His narrowed gaze soldered on her brilliant smile. Who was the blasted woman smiling at *now?* She wasn't still dancing with Aaron Black. This guy had lighter hair, broader shoulders, wasn't quite so tall…Justin's stomach muscles suddenly unclenched. It was Matt. She was just dancing with Matt Walker, and although God knew the rancher was known to turn more than one single woman's eye, he was also a member of the Club. A friend.

Still, that didn't mean Justin had to like the way he was holding Win. Or smiling at her, for that damn matter. There was a limit to loyalty and friendship. Come to think of it, there was a limit to loyalty and friendship and honor and ethics.

And that damn limit was Winona Raye.

Aw, hell. He was losing his mind. It was her. She'd always made him lose his mind, and every year it was getting worse. He was beginning to sound like a lovesick cow. More pathetic yet, he was beginning to act like one.

"Hey, Dr. Webb, can I get you another?"

Justin's head snapped around. ''Sure, Riley. I'd appreciate a refill.'' Well aware he'd been acting—and thinking—way too soberly for a party, he offered a companionable grin for Riley Monroe and another for the stranger next to him.

The short gentleman offered his hand. ''I believe that we met on one other occasion, Dr. Webb. My name is Klimt. Robert Klimt.''

''Oh, yes. Of course, I remember.'' Actually Justin had no memory of the man whatsoever, but he scrounged his brain for some connection. Klimt, Klimt…he was almost sure somebody'd told him that Robert Klimt was a minor cabinet member in the Asterland government.

''I was just asking Mr. Monroe about the sign over the entrance door.'' Klimt motioned to the Leadership, Justice and Peace logo. ''I heard someone say that slogan came from a historical story about the town. I gather that there's some kind of romantic legend about Royal, Texas, and some jewels?''

''Oh, there is, there is.'' Riley topped off Justin's glass with a flourish, then reached behind the bar for Klimt's poison—imported schnapps. ''Next door to our Texas Cattleman's Club here is a park. You probably noticed. In the early 1800s, there was a mission here, an old adobe church. It's just part of the park now, but back in the War with Mexico, 1846 or so, there was a Texas soldier found a comrade fallen in battle, tried to save him….''

The fiddlers had picked up the pace for ''The Yellow Rose of Texas.'' Justin, half listening to Klimt and Riley, researched the dance floor for the black, bouncing curly hair again. She wasn't with Aaron, wasn't with Matthew. In a sense, she really *was* working this evening, even if she was wearing formal attire. Win had never been a carry-a-gun kind of cop—she normally worked with juveniles, kids in trouble, kids at risk. But everyone on the local police force had been quietly coaxed to attend the gathering tonight, because the whole town wanted this shindig to go well, and Winona was always pulled into special problems like this. She was ideal. Everyone knew her. Everyone trusted her. And that was just great, except that she was so damned beautiful, Justin figured some guy, sometime, was going to zip down those cool defenses of hers....

"... So anyhow, this Texas soldier was just trying to save a wounded comrade, but it was just too late. Our Texas soldier had no idea the guy was carrying these three fancy jewels until he's caring for the body, trying to bury him. Anyway, the old guy was gone, no identification on him, so he took the jewels back to Royal—"

"And this is a true story?" Klimt asked.

Justin yanked his gaze off the dance floor and looked at Klimt again. The man couldn't be five foot five, but for a little guy, he sure had the puff of a banty rooster. Everything about him was starched—posture stiff as a ramrod, linen shirt perfectly creased, hair perfectly brushed, smile perfectly appropriate. Even his shoes shone like mirrors. Justin's glance strayed to the smaller man's left temple. There was a mole there, right by his eye. There were beauty marks, and then there were moles. This happened to be a plain old ugly mole—Justin immediately looked away; it was just second nature as a doc to notice a precancerous physical condition. And in this case, the minor flaw was particularly striking because everything about the guy was so spiffed-up-perfect in every other way.

Riley was laughing. "Aw, none of the story is true. Or maybe it is. The truth is that none of us seem to care. The town loves the legend, so we've been passing it on for years."

"So tell me more about these jewels," Klimt requested.

"Well, to start with, each of the jewels refers to the motto on the Texas Cattleman's Club sign, see? Each of the gems is really unusual, partly because they're so rare as to be priceless. You couldn't buy one for love or money, not then and not now. Which made it all the more interesting and mysterious, why this Texas soldier was carrying them—but we'll never know that answer. The point is that he had them. And one stone was a red diamond—''

''I never heard that diamonds came in a red color.''

''They don't, they don't,'' Riley said. ''Except once in a real rare while. And you study some gem lore, now, and you find red diamonds were the stones of kings, because they were that rare. So you look up in our motto sign, and that's what the first word—*leadership*—is about. That's what the red diamond is a symbol for. Right, Dr. Webb?''

''Right, Riley.'' The orchestra had switched tunes to an old-fashioned waltz. Aaron Black glided past with a tall, plain young woman in his arms. Justin thought he recognized her. Pamela something? A teacher? Very shy, very proper— and how typical of Aaron to pick out a wallflower and make sure she wasn't pining on the sidelines.

Even better that he wasn't dancing with Win. Justin searched the crowd again. He saw Aaron, he saw Matt, he saw... *Finally,* he caught a glimpse of her again. This time she was partnered by a man with coal-black hair and striking gray eyes, teeth shining stark white in a face that so rarely smiled—the Sheikh. Ben. And another Texas Cattleman's Club member, thank God, so it wasn't like Justin had to worry she wasn't in a gentleman's hands.

Exactly.

He trusted Ben the same way he trusted Aaron and Matt. With his life. But trusting them with a single, attractive woman was a different story—particularly when the men had no idea how much he cared about her.

Nor would they.

''Dr. Webb, Mr. Klimt was asking about the other stones....'' Riley prompted him.

''Yeah? Well, the legend has it that there's the red diamond...and then a black harlequin opal...and then an emerald.''

''Yeah, yeah,'' Riley agreed, and settled on his elbows on

the bar to keep spinning the tale for his willing listener. "See, technically the opal's the least valuable of the three stones. But a black harlequin opal—she's a rare mother. And those who get into the magic of gems tend to see the harlequin opal as both having healing power and as somehow having the inner light and power to bring justice—so that's where the second word in the Club motto comes from. *Justice.* As an ideal, you know?"

"Yes, Mr. Monroe, I believe I know what an ideal is," Klimt said impatiently. "And the third stone, the emerald?"

"I'm coming to that one. Around the world, for centuries, emeralds were always considered the stone of peacemakers, and this particular emerald was said to be one giant stone besides. So *peace* was naturally the third word they put in the Club motto."

"Leadership, justice, peace," Klimt echoed. "That's quite a story. But it seems such an elaborate legend if the stones never really existed."

"And there's more to it than that," Riley said happily. "Our guy brought the stones back to Royal after the war with Mexico. He was gonna be rich, you know, sell 'em, buy a big spread, put up a fancy house and all? And he meant to, only he got home, and oil was found on his homestead. He had black gold coming out of his ears, so he never did need to sell those stones to have his fortune made."

"So what happened to them?"

Riley peered over Justin's glass, then Klimt's, then ducked down to bring up bottles again. "I don't know. Nobody knows. The Texas Cattleman's Club...well, there were some men formed this group, back even before Club founder Tex Langley's time. Some say they first got together to guard the jewels. Some say they were just the leading citizens of Royal, who passed on responsibility for the town's security from generation to generation. Some say they just used the legend of the jewels to create that motto, because, well, it was a good motto. Those are our values around here. Leadership. Justice. Pea—''

''You think the jewels exist?''

Riley fingered his chest. ''Me? Oh, you bet. I think they existed for real, back then, and they exist somewhere now.''

''So what do you think happened to them?''

''Well, everybody's got a theory....''

Someone cut in on her with the Sheikh. Dakota Lewis. Justin's eyes tracked the two of them on the dance floor, and he almost had to smile. Dakota wasn't much on dancing. Win'd be lucky if she left the floor without broken toes if she stuck with him long. Dakota looked what he was—no uniform, but the retired military status was obvious from his unyielding posture and scalped haircut. On the surface he looked tough and hard—and truth to tell he was—but Justin couldn't worry about Winona with Dakota. Since his divorce, Dakota had shown no interest in any women.

''Well, if the jewels *did* exist, where is your best guess they'd be hidden?'' Klimt asked Riley.

Again Justin turned his head to the other two men. Klimt could only seem to march to one drummer. The town loved its legend. Actually, outsiders seemed to love it just as much; tourists consistently ate it up. But Klimt was pushing it beyond anyone's normal interest. ''If the jewels really existed, they'd be under heavy lock and key,'' he said mildly. ''We only encourage the legend because it's good fun for everyone. And who'd want to be the one to break hearts by confessing that Santa Claus didn't exist? I sure plan to believe until I'm 110.''

Riley chortled appreciatively. ''You saying you believe in Santa or the jewels, Dr. Webb?''

''In Santa, of course. You can have the jewels. I'll take the loot Santa carries around any day.''

Riley laughed again. Klimt even threw him a sour smile, and, temporarily, Riley seemed to be off the hook for entertaining Mr. Banty Rooster. Klimt, carrying a fresh schnapps, wandered off into the crowd.

And Justin was about to do that, too…until Winona caught his attention again. She was still on the dance floor, but dancing with a stranger this time.

A non-Texan. One of the Asterlanders that Justin didn't know. He watched the dude's big hand sift down to her fanny.

She smiled at the guy. And then reached back and removed his hand.

Justin shifted on his feet. Something kicked in his pulse. Not just jealousy—God knew he knew all the shades of green there were in that particularly annoying emotion. But Winona was clearly handling the guy—no matter how protective Justin felt, the truth was, he'd never seen a man that Winona couldn't handle with both hands tied.

That was, in fact, why she so often got conned into attending these kinds of shindigs. Regular cops were always around for security, but it wasn't the same. The few serious crimes in Royal tended to be robbery. Sure, there was a crime of passion now and then, a fight at the Royal Diner occasionally, domestic dispute problems and that sort of thing. But basically this just wasn't a high-crime community. This was oil country. Those who'd made it, made it big. And those who hadn't made it were paid well, simply because there was ample to go around. The school systems were top-drawer, the whole area supported with fine services. The only ''risk'' prevalent in a small, ultrarich town like Royal was its being a draw for thieves.

Which was exactly why and how Winona was irreplaceable at these galas. She always showed up in the same evil black dress, the same sassy high heels. It wasn't that she showed off anything—ever—but there just didn't seem to be a man born who wouldn't talk to her. On top of that, she sensed things. She had an intuition when someone or something wasn't right.

And Justin frowned again suddenly. No guy was eyeing her at that specific moment—and her dance partner had quit trying to put the make on her. But her gaze was roving the room. She tripped in her partner's arms—which wasn't that much of a shock, because unless a man let her lead, she couldn't dance worth a Texas jumping bean. But it was the way she suddenly moved—stiffly, warily—that had Justin suddenly alert and pushing through bodies to get to the other side of the room.

Maybe she didn't know he was in love with her.

Maybe she'd never think of him as anything more than the old friend she'd grown up with.

For damn sure, maybe she'd never realize that his offers to marry her were sincere.

But if Winona were in trouble, Justin was going to be there for her—whether she wanted him there or not.

Two

Winona was in such trouble.

She'd slept with the same dream two nights running, replaying the evening of the Texas Cattleman's Club gala. She *knew* it was just another dream, because the same details kept getting embellished. In the dream, she was breathtakingly gorgeous—which was a lot of fun, but not remotely realistic. She'd been whirling and swirling on the dance floor, not tripping, being graceful—which was another reason she knew it was a dream. And she kept dancing with different men— man after man after man, all of them adorable, all of them charmed by every word that came out of her mouth, fighting to have another spin with her around the floor....

Okay, okay, so these were pretty ridiculous dreams. But they were *her* dreams, and she was having a great time with them.

Only in this particular night's version, Justin pulled her into his arms. For "The Tennessee Waltz"—which had to be one of the schmaltziest songs of all time, a song doomed to bring out romantic feelings in even the toughest of women—such as herself—and suddenly she was naked. Whirling around the floor. Waltzing. Without a stitch on. Only being naked was okay, because there wasn't a soul in the room who realized that she was naked. Except for herself.

And Justin.

Alarm bells started clanging in her ears, but Winona determinedly ignored them. Obviously this wasn't real, and since this happened to be her personal, wicked dream, she didn't want to let go of it until she had to.

Justin couldn't take his eyes off her. She whacked him upside the head—which was such a real, logical thing for her to do that for a second, Winona freaked that this wasn't a dream—but he didn't seem to mind, and the whack didn't seem to stop him from looking, either…a long, slow look that began with her naked toes, dawdled past long slender legs (this was a dream, for sure), past hips without a single spare ounce of fat on them (and a damn *good* dream), up, his gaze a caress that took in waist and proud, trembling breasts and white throat, then up to her vulnerable, naked eyes.

Yeah, she wanted him.

She'd always wanted him.

Another alarm bell clanged in her mind—but for Pete's sake, in the privacy of a dream, a girl should be able to be honest with herself. Justin looked like a young Sam Elliot. Tall. Lanky. With a slow, lazy drawl and a lot for a girl to worry about in those sexy eyes. Cover those broad shoulders in a tux and a woman just wanted to sip him in—correction—sip him in and lap him up both.

A vague memory surfaced in her dream. She'd been twelve. Until she'd been fostered with the Gerard family, she'd never had a bike, and she was new to the family, still waiting for someone to hit her, someone to scold her. It'd happen. She just didn't know when yet, but she was wary this time, prepared to protect herself. She didn't need anybody to watch out for her...it was just the bike. Oh man, oh man, she wanted to ride a bike so badly, and everybody assumed she knew how, at her age. But she didn't. And the first time she took it out, it was almost dusk, because no one was on the street then, no strangers to see her.

And Justin had been there when she'd crashed into a tree. Helped her up. Righted the bike. A gorgeous heartthrob of a seventeen-year-old—with a chivalrous streak—enough to make her tough, hard, mean, cold heart go *hoboyhoboyhoboy*. He'd touched her cheek. Made her laugh. Then she'd had to punch him for helping her, of course. What else could a twelve-year-old do?

More alarm bells clanged in her mind. The same, annoying, insistent alarm bells.

Winona's eyes popped open on a pitch-black bedroom. She wasn't twelve and falling into a sinking-deep, mortifying crush with Justin Webb. She wasn't dancing naked with Justin at the Texas Cattleman's Club, either. It was just her bedroom, and the telephone was ringing off the hook, at seven in the morning—according to the insane neon dials on the bedside clock.

The instant she read the time, though, she snapped awake fast. There was only one reason for a telephone call at this crazy hour. Trouble. And although technically she was a nine-to-five cop, working with at-risk teens, reality was that kids never got in trouble at nice, convenient hours.

She fumbled for the lamp switch, then hit the ground running, shagging a hand through her tousled hair as she grabbed the receiver.

"Winona?"

Not a kid. An adult's voice. Her boss, from the precinct. "You know it's me. What's wrong, Wayne?"

"You know the jet that was supposed to take off last night for Asterland? The hotsy totsy flight with all the royalty and dignitaries and all?"

"Yes, of course." So did the whole town.

"Well, something went wrong. She lifted off, barely got in the air before they were radioing in some garbled, panicked message about a problem. Next thing, they're making an emergency landing about fifteen miles out of town, middle of nowhere, flat as a pancake. Fire broke out—"

She got the gist. The details didn't matter. "Holy cow. How can I help?"

"Truthfully, I don't know." Winona could well imagine Wayne squinting and rubbing the back of his head. He didn't like trouble in his town. The way Wayne saw it, Royal belonged to him. Anyone took the crease out of those jeans ticked him off. "I'm calling from the scene. Everything's a mess. This all just happened less than a half hour ago. First thing was getting everybody off the plane safely. Only a couple seem badly injured, the rest are just shaken. But what the hell happened, I don't know. And I don't want every Tom, Dick and curious Harry messing with my crime scene. It's still dark. Only so much I can get done until daylight—"

He was talking more to himself than to her. Winona knew how her boss's mind worked. "So where could I be the most help? At the hospital? The plane site? The office?"

"Here," Wayne said bluntly. "You gonna kick me straight to Austin if I admit I just want a woman here?"

"Probably." Holding the phone clamped to her ear with one hand, she reached for the deodorant on the dresser and thumbed open the lid. Applying deodorant one-handed was tricky, but she'd done it before.

"Well, then, you're just going to have to kick me. To be honest, everything's being handled that needs to be. It's just, that ain't good enough. Not for this. Dad blame it, we seem to have the makings of a major international incident. First, we have a plane that I'm told is top of the line, perfect, nothing can go wrong—but it still crash-landed. Then we have embassies calling. We have Washington calling. We've got fire trucks from Midland to Odessa joining in to help us. Then half the town—naturally—is starting to show up as the sun comes up, it's like trying to stop an avalanche. Next thing the women'll be bringing casseroles. It's a madhouse. We *got* to find out what caused this plane crash and to do that, we have to get everybody out of here and get some kind of order. I just want my whole team here, that's all. Even if—''

''Wayne?''

''What?''

''Stop talking. Give me directions.'' He did. ''I'll be there in twenty minutes.'' She hung up and started moving. Plucked white panties from the drawer, pulled them on, then hopped into low-rise, boot-cut jeans. She stood up, head scrambled. Not by Wayne's call in itself. Maybe she was hired to work only with juveniles, but this wasn't some big eastern city. This was Texas. People pitched in whenever there was a crisis, and no one gave a rat's toenail over whether helping fit a job description.

But a plane crash-landing was big news—and troubling. She knew every single face that had been on that flight— they'd all been at the Texas Cattleman's Club gala two nights ago—and a few of them were personal friends of hers besides. Pamela Miles had been flying to Asterland to be an exchange teacher. Lady Helena had made herself known around town because she was the kind to involve herself in caring causes. On top of that…well, the whole world was troubling these days, but not Royal. Things just didn't happen here. Sure, there were some thefts and squabbles and people who lost their screws now and then, but nothing unusual. Nothing happened there that would ever draw attention from outsiders.

Suddenly she heard a sound—a sound odd and unexpected enough to make her quit jogging down the hall and stop for a second. The sound had seemed like a mewling baby's cry— but of course, that was ridiculous. When she heard nothing again, she picked up her pace.

In the peach-and-cream kitchen, she flicked on the light, started her espresso machine, then peeled back toward her bedroom, mentally cataloguing what she still had to do. She needed coffee, her hair brushed, an apple for the road, and yeah, something to wear above the waist. She never wore a uniform—if you were going to dress for success with kids, you wore jeans and no symbols or labels to put them off— but that wasn't to say she could arrive at a crash site topless. There were times she fantasized about giving Wayne an attack of apoplexy—God knew her boss was a hard-core chauvinist—but not today.

She pulled a sports bra over her head, burrowed in a drawer for an old black sweater…then jerked her head up again.

Damn. Somewhere there *was* a sound. An off-kilter, didn't-belong-in-her-house sound. A puppy crying? A cat lost in the neighborhood somewhere nearby?

Silently, still listening, she straightened the sweater, pulled on socks, shoved her feet into boots, grabbed a brush. Her hair looked like a squirrel's nest, but then that's how it looked when it was freshly styled, too. A glance at her face in the bathroom mirror somehow, inexplicably, made her think of Justin again…and that dream in which his gaze had been all over her naked body.

She scowled in the mirror. First, strange dreams, then strange sounds—she'd seemed to wake up in la la land today, and on a morning when she needed to be her sharpest.

Swiftly she thumbed off the light and started hustling for real. In the kitchen, she poured coffee, then backtracked to the hall closet for her jacket, scooping up the stuff she needed: car keys, an apple, a lid for her espresso, some money for lunch. Almost the minute she finished collecting her debris, her feet seemed to be instinctively making a detour. One minute. That's all she needed to check all the rooms and make absolutely positive that nothing was making that odd sound from inside the house. It wasn't as if she lived in a mighty mansion that would take hours to check out. Her ranch-style house was downright miniscule—but it was hers. Hers and the bank's, anyway.

She'd put a chunky down payment on it last year. She was twenty-eight, time to stop renting. Time to start making sure she had a place and security and in a neighborhood with a lot of kids and a good school system. Her bedroom was cobalt-blue and white, and, since decorating choices scared her, she'd just used the same colors in the bathroom. A second bedroom she used as a den, where she stashed her TV and computer—and anything she didn't have time to put away. The third bedroom was the biggest, and stood starkly empty—Winona wasn't admitting the room was intended for a baby, not to anyone, at least not yet. But it was.

The kitchen was a non-cook's dream, practical, with lots of make-easy machines and tools, the counters and walls covered with warm peach tiles that led down into the living room. A cocoa couch viewed the backyard, bird feeders all over the place, lots of windows…*damn*. There, she heard the sound again. The mewling cry.

Either that or she was going out of her mind, which, of course, was always a possibility. But she unlatched the front door and yanked it open.

Her jaw surely dropped ten feet. Her ranch house was white adobe, with redbrick arches in the doorways. And there, in the doorway shadow, was a wicker laundry basket. The basket appeared to be stuffed with someone's old, clean laundry, rags and sheets…but damned if that wasn't where the crying sound emanated from.

The car keys slipped from her fingers and clattered to the cold steps. The apple slipped from her other hand and rolled down the drive, forgotten. She hunched down, quickly parting the folds and creases of fabric.

When she saw the baby, her heart stopped.

Abandoned. The baby had actually been abandoned.

"Ssh, ssh, it's all right, don't cry…." So carefully, so gingerly, she lifted out the little one. The morning was icy

at the edges, the light still a predawn-gray. The baby was too
swathed in torn-up blankets and rags to clearly make out its
features or anything else.

"Ssh, ssh," Winona kept crooning, but her heart was
slamming, slamming. Feelings seeped through her nerves,
through her heart from a thousand long-locked doors, bub-
bled up to the pain of naked air. She'd been abandoned as a
child. She knew what an abandoned child felt like...and
would feel like, her whole life.

A crinkle of paper slipped out of the basket. It only took
Winona a few seconds to read the printed message.

Dear Winona Raye,
I have no way to take care of my Angel. You are the
only one I could ask. Please love her.

Winona's cop experience immediately registered several
things—that there'd be no way to track the generic paper and
ordinary print, that the writing was simple but not unedu-
cated, and that somehow the mother of the baby knew her
specifically—well enough to identify her name, and well
enough to believe she was someone who would care for a
baby.

Which, God knows, she would.

As swiftly as Winona read the note, she put it aside. There
was no time for that now. The baby was wet beneath the
blankets, the morning biting at the January-freezing temper-
atures. She scooped up the little one and hustled inside the
warm house, rocking, crooning, whispering reassurances...all
past the gulp in her throat that had to be bigger than the state
of Texas.

God knew what she was going to do. But right now nothing mattered but the obvious. Taking care of the child. Making sure the little one was warm, dry, fed, healthy. Then
Winona would try to figure out why anyone would have left

the baby on her doorstep specifically...and all the other issues about what the child's circumstances might be.

That fast, that instantaneously, Win felt a bond with the baby that wrapped around her heart tighter than a vise. The thing was, as little as she knew—she already knew too much.

She was already positive that the child was going to get thrown in the foster-care system, because that's what happened when a child was deserted. Even if a parent immediately showed up, the court would still place the child in the care of Social Services—at least temporarily—because whatever motivated the parent to abandon the child could mean it wasn't safe in their care. A change of heart wasn't enough. An investigation needed to be conducted to establish what the child's circumstances were.

Winona knew all those legal procedures—both from her job and from her life. And although she knew her feelings were irrational—and annoyingly emotional—it didn't stop the instinct of bonding. The fierceness of caring. The instantaneous heart surge—even panic—to protect this baby better than she'd been protected. To save this baby the way she almost hadn't been saved. To love this baby the way—to be honest—Winona never had been and never expected to be loved.

There were several coffee machines spread through Royal Memorial Hospital, but only one that counted. After he'd switched from trauma medicine to plastic surgery, Justin had generally tried to avoid the Emergency Room, but by ten that morning, he was desperate. Groggy-eyed, he pushed the coins into the machine, punched his choice of Straight Black, kicked the base—he knew this coffee machine intimately— and then waited.

He wasn't standing there three minutes before he got a series of claps and thumps on his back. It was, "Hey, Dr. Webb, slumming down here?" and "Hi, Doc, we sure miss you" and "Dr. Webb, it's nice to see you with us again."

As soon as he could yank the steaming cup out of the machine, he gulped a sip. Burned all the way down. The taste was more familiar than his own heartbeat. Battery acid, more bitter than sludge, and liberally laced with caffeine.

Fantastic.

He inhaled another gulp, and then aimed straight ahead. Down the hall, through the double glass doors, was his Plastic Surgery/Burn Unit. The community believed that the wing had been anonymously donated, which was fine with Justin. What mattered to him was that in two short years, the unit had already developed the reputation for being the best in the state. He couldn't ask for more. The equipment was the best and the technology the newest. The walls were ice-blue, the atmosphere sterile, serene, quiet. Perfect.

Nothing like the chaotic loony bin in the ER. Royal Memorial was a well-run small hospital, but a crisis stretched the capacity of its trauma unit—and the crash landing of the Asterland jet earlier that morning was still stressing the trauma team. Nobody'd had time to pick up towels and drapes. Staff jogged past in blood- and debris-stained coats. A kid squealed past him. A shrieking mom was trying to chase the kid. A nurse trailed both of them, looking harassed and taking mother-may-I giant steps. He heard babies' cries, codes on the loudspeaker. Lights flashed; phones rang; carts wheeled and wheedled past. Somebody'd spilled a coffee; someone else had thrown up, so those stinks added to all the other messes and noises. Just being around it all made something clutch in his chest. Something cruel and sharp.

Justin loved his Plastic Surgery/Burn Unit. He made a difference in his Burn Unit, for God's sake. He wanted nothing to do with trauma medicine anymore. Nothing.

He sucked down another gulp of sludge, and this time aimed down the hall and refused to look back...but he suddenly caught sight of the top of a curly-haired head coming out of a side room.

"Winona?" He wanted to shake himself. One look at

her—that's all it took—and his hormones line-danced the length of his nerves and sashayed back again. At least he promptly forgot his old hunger for the ER. "Win?"

Her head jerked up when she heard his voice. That was the first he noticed that she was carrying a baby—not that there was anything all that unusual about Winona being stuck with a kid in the Emergency Room. Her job often put her in the middle between a child and school or parents. But something about her expression alerted Justin that this was nothing like an average day for Win.

Her smile for him, though, was as natural and familiar as sunshine. "I figured you'd be in the thick of this," she said wryly. "What a morning, huh? Were you out at the site of the crash landing?"

"Yeah, first thing. I'm not one of the doctors on call for something like that, but you know how fast news travels in Royal. I got a call, someone who'd heard there was a fire associated with the crash—so I hightailed it out there, too. I'll tell you, it was a real chaotic scene. But any outsider was just in the way, so all I did was the obvious, help the trauma team get patients routed back here. Particularly those going into my Burn Unit."

Her eyes promptly sobered. "I haven't heard anything about how many serious injuries there were yet. Was it bad?"

Something had happened to her. Justin had no more time for idle chitchat than he suspected she did, but he kept talking, because it gave him a chance to look her over. His gaze roved from the crown of her head to her toes—the way the jeans cupped her fanny, the boots, her wildly tousled hair, the way her cheeks had pinked from the slap of a cold morning wind—none of that was unusual. But there was something different in her eyes. A fever-brightness. She stood there, rocking, rocking the bundle in her arms—the baby made no sound at all—but that liquid softness in Win's eyes was rare. Vulnerable. And Winona just never looked vulnerable if she could help it.

A blood cart pushed between them, but he wasn't about to stop their conversation just because all hell was still breaking loose. "Things could have been a lot worse. At least no one died. In a crash landing, that's pretty much a miracle in itself. Robert Klimt—one of the minor cabinet members from Asterland? He was knocked unconscious, head injury—I don't know how he is right now, I took care of some minor burns and left him to the neurologist. Pamela Miles was also on that flight—"

"I know, I know! She was headed overseas to be an exchange teacher in Asterland—did you see her, Justin? Do you know if she's okay?"

"I didn't take care of her myself, but I heard she was basically fine. Lady Helena, though—"

"Serious injuries?"

"Well, not life-threatening. Complicated break in her ankle. And once she's done with the bone man, for sure she's going to be mine. She did get some burns—"

"Oh, God. She's such a beautiful woman."

Justin couldn't say more on Helena. For him to discuss a patient, any patient—he just never did. Not with anyone, even Winona. But he still hadn't taken his eyes off her and didn't want to give her the excuse to shoot past him. "Well, at this point, I think everyone on the flight's been through here, checked out, even if they seemed to be fine. And the whole town was as shook up as the passengers on that flight, it seems like, because people were flooding in right and left."

"You didn't hear what caused the emergency landing, did you?"

On that he had to lift his eyebrows. "I was just going to ask *you* that, Ms. Police Officer. If anyone had answers, I figure it would be the cops first."

"Well, normally I'd be elbowing my way to the middle of the mess from the start," she admitted wryly, "but I got sidetracked."

When she lifted the corner of the pale pink flannel blanket

for him to get a peek, Justin finally figured out what the emotion was in her eyes. Fierceness. The fierce protectiveness of a mama lion for her cub, or a mama eagle for her eaglet. There was nothing strange about thinking of Win and motherhood, or of her wanting to be a mom, but it just hadn't crossed his mind before what a major thing it might be for her. His knuckles—almost accidentally—brushed her hand when he touched the baby's cheek.

"Don't tell me anyone hurt this darling, or I'll have to go out and kill someone," he said gently.

Her voice melted. "Oh, God. Justin. That's exactly how I felt. Isn't she beautiful?"

Considering she was swaddled up with nothing showing but about two inches of face and some blond spriggy hairs, Justin was hard-pressed to use the word *beautiful*. On the baby. "What's the story?"

"Her name's Angel. I ran out my front door this morning, headed for the crash site—Wayne called me around seven in the morning—and there she was. In a basket on the doorstep. With a note saying her name was Angel and asking me, specifically, to take care of her."

Justin felt his pulse still. "This isn't the first time you've had to handle an abandoned kid," he said carefully.

"No, of course not. But this baby's so young that obviously I had to bring her here first. I'm sure you know the beat. This day and age, a deserted baby could mean drugs or AIDS or all kinds of things in the child's background—so before we can do anything else, we have to know the state of the child's health for sure."

"And…?"

"And Dr. Julian gave her a terrific bill of health. Just under three months old, he thought. "

"So, the next step is…?" He was watching her face, not the baby's.

"Finding the mother, of course. It's not like Royal is that huge. And if anyone has a bird's-eye view to kids in trouble, it's got to be me in my job. So if anyone can track down the parents, I've got the best shot.''

''Uh-huh. And where will the baby go in the meantime?''

Her head shot up. Blue eyes blazed on his. ''I spent years in foster care,'' she said belligerently.

''I know you did.''

''The system's overcrowded. Even in an area this wealthy, there's no answer for it. Adoption is at least a possibility for a blond, blue-eyed baby—but not for this one, not for some time. Even if I run a hundred miles an hour and get answers zip-fast, there's still no way to rush a—''

''Win, you sound like you're fighting with a judge in a court of law. You're just talking to me. What's the deal here? I take it you want to keep the baby?''

Her shoulders sank, losing all that tough stiffness. And again her eyes got that softness, that terribly fierce vulnerability that he'd never seen before. ''No one's going to let me keep her. I'm single. And I'm working full-time besides. But right now—especially today—the town's in chaos because of the Asterland jet crash. So the only thing that makes sense—''

Justin heard his code paged on the loudspeaker. An orderly pushed past both of them to clean up the examining room. Bodies were still hustling in both directions, they were blocking the hallway—and the baby suddenly opened her rosebud mouth, yawned, and blinked open sleepy, priceless, exquisite blue eyes.

He looked at the baby...and then at Winona again. ''We've both got our hands full right now,'' he said casually. ''How about if I stop by for a short visit right after dinner?''

''You don't have to do that.''

Oh yeah, he thought, he definitely did.

Three

Just as Winona lifted a fork to her mouth, she heard the baby's thin cry. Somehow there'd been no time for lunch. Now it looked as if the odds weren't too hot on sneaking some dinner, either. Not that she minded. Who needed food? Dropping the fork with a clatter, she charged toward the living room. "I'm coming, Angel! I'm coming!"

Well, shoot. It wasn't quite that easy—as a woman or a temporary mom—to deliver on those optimistic words. Although it was only the distance of a fast gallop between the kitchen and the living room, reaching the baby was becoming more challenging by the hour.

She'd only called a couple of neighbors that afternoon, but it seemed that the news about the baby had spread and help had been pouring in nonstop. The whole neighborhood was kid-studded—which was one of the reasons she'd chosen to buy her house here—and almost everyone had some baby gear stored in their garages or back rooms. Buying anything would have been silly: Winona had no idea how long she would be allowed to keep the baby. But her neighbors' loans had been extravagantly generous. She had to dodge a half-dozen car seats, a couple of high chairs, several playpens and walkers, backpacks, front packs, diaper bags, toys, enough blankets to warm a child in the Arctic, and heaps of baby clothes. Finally she reached the white wicker bassinet with the pink quilted lining.

Inside was the princess, who happened to be garbed in her fifth outfit of the day. Winona figured they surely wouldn't go through quite so many clothes tomorrow. She was getting close to mastering disposable diapers.

''There, there. There, there....'' She picked up the precious bundle, and started the crooning, patting and rocking movements that seemed to be the eternal song of mothers. But on the inside, panic started to ooze through her nerves.

''Are we hungry, sweetheart? Wet? Do you want the TV on? Off? More lights, less lights? More noise, less noise? Are you cold? Constipated—no, come to think of it, I'm positive that's not a problem. Are you mad? Bored? Sick? Sad? Whatever it is, I'll fix it, I swear. Just don't cry. There, there. There, there, love....''

The panic was new. All day, she'd been in seventh heaven. Babies had been on her heart's agenda for a long time, and no, of course Angel wasn't hers and wasn't likely to be for long. Winona was trying her best to be completely realistic about that. It was just...carrying the little one around had seemed as natural as breathing. There'd been a thousand things to do, starting with taking the baby to the hospital for a checkup, then carting her back to the station, talking to Wayne, then claiming some computer time, then calling some moms in the neighborhood before stopping at a store for supplies. The busier she was, the more the baby seemed to love it. But then they'd come home.

Alone.

And Angel had lived up to her name tag all day until, it sure seemed, the point when Winona realized she *was* alone with the baby. And knew nothing about child care. The baby had barely let out a peep all day, but now she seemed to be scaling up every few minutes. The darling either desperately missed her real mother, or Angel had suddenly figured out that she was stuck with a complete rookie.

The doorbell rang. Winona whipped around, thinking, please, God, not another car seat or another well-meant baby blanket. Hunger was starting to set in. Exhaustion.

A nightmare-strength panic.

Before she could reach the front door, the knob rattled and Justin poked his head in. Her pulse promptly soared ten feet. There was no stopping it. So typically, even after a long workday, he looked as revved as the satin-black Porsche in her drive. He stepped in like a vital burst of energy, his face wind-stung, his eyes snapping life, his grin teasing her before he'd even said a word. "Win? Are you there—well, I can see you're there. And a little on the busy side, huh?"

"I never thought you meant it about coming over! Come in, come in!" She wished she'd had a chance to brush her hair and put on lipstick, but what was the difference? It was just Justin. And no matter how mercilessly he ended up teasing her, she was thrilled to see him. "What do you know about babies?" she called over the caterwauling.

"Nothing."

Never mind. She didn't care what he knew or didn't know. She closed the door with him firmly on the inside. He was still another body. She wasn't alone. "You're a doctor, you have to know something—"

"Yeah, I've been trying to tell my patients that for a long time." He peeled off his sheepskin jacket, took a step toward her living room and froze. "Holy cow. Did you have a cattle drive in here this afternoon?"

"Very funny. It's just baby gear. Loans from the neighbors. Now listen, Justin, whether you know anything or not— you could hold her for a second, couldn't you? I just need a minute. Time to get some dry diapers and fresh clothes and a bottle warmed up—''

''Okay.''

''It won't take me long to do any of that stuff—''

''Okay.''

''Don't panic because she's crying. She's really a darling. I just have to figure out what's wrong. That's all there is to it. You figure out what's wrong, you fix it, she quits—''

''Hey, Win. Could you try and believe it's okay? I really did come over to help.''

It's not that she didn't believe Justin. It was just that his offer to help seemed so unlikely. The town may have labeled Justin a devil-may-care bachelor, but Winona had always known better than that. Something had happened to him in Bosnia, because he'd come back a different person—quieter, more closed in, and he'd left his once-loved trauma medicine specialty in favor of plastic surgery. But his reputation as a surgeon spanned the southwest. His participation with the Texas Cattleman's Club was another unrecognized involvement. And she'd never forgotten meeting him back when she was twelve, on the first day she'd been fostered with the Gerards. To her, he'd been the best-looking teenage guy in the universe. Even that young, he'd had the sexiest eyes. The laziest drawl in Texas. A way of looking at a woman. And a way of picking up a little girl—and her bike—from the sidewalk, and somehow making her skinned pride feel better in spite of impossible odds.

Most of their relationship, though, he'd been an inescapable, nonstop tease. He'd shown up to check out the guy who'd taken her to the senior prom, had a conniption fit when she sunned in a bikini, regularly asked her to marry him as if he thought that was funny, taught her to drive stick shift, and damnation, held her head when she'd come home from a party after her first (and last) experience with rum-and-colas. Short and sweet, he'd been a friend in her life forever—when he wasn't being insufferable. And it was forgetting that "insufferable" adjective that was tough for her.

"What do you mean, you came over to help?" she asked suspiciously.

"Just what I said." He scooped the baby out of her arms. "Right now, though, we don't have a prayer of talking over the sound of Ms. Bawler. Go. Do the bottle thing. And I'll try and figure out the diapers if you'll steer me toward the supplies."

Her hand shot to her chest. A mere twenty-eight and she was almost having a heart attack. "You're volunteering to change a diaper? Have you had these symptoms long? Are you suffering from fever? Brain tumor? A history of lunacy you never mentioned before?"

For those insults, he tousled her hair—as if it wasn't already a royal mess—before walking off with the baby. The phone rang six times over the next hour, and two more neighbors stopped by bearing car seats and blankets. But somehow all the confusion and running wasn't the same with Justin there. The terror factor had disappeared. Contrary to his claims of inexperience, he acted like a veteran with both diaper sticky tabs and burping. And Angel seemed to forget that she was ticked off at the world in general. At the first sound of his voice, she started blowing bubbles and drooling.

"Just like all the other women in town," Winona muttered.

"Pardon?"

"I said the baby fell in love with you from the first instant you picked her up."

"Yeah, I noticed she quit crying. You think she recognizes a good-looking guy, young as she is? Someone with class and taste and brilliance—hey!"

As hard as she'd tossed the couch pillow at his head, he just pushed it aside with a grin. By then it was around eight o'clock. Angel had not only been fed, burped and changed, but she'd settled down in the bassinet. Winona couldn't quite remember when Justin had ordered her to sit on the cocoa couch and pushed a hot plate of food in her hands, but she finally seemed to have caught some dinner; she was slouched down like a lazy slug and one stockinged foot was keeping the bassinet-rocker in motion.

Justin—for the first and likely only time in the universe—was kneeling at her feet. She'd felt obligated to mention, several times, how much she approved of his kneeling position. "It's really where all men belong. In a submissive position to their superiors—meaning we women, of course. Waiting on us. Obeying us. Working to please us—"

"If you don't cut it out, I'm going to have to get up and tickle you. Then you'll start laughing and screaming. Then you'll risk waking the baby—"

"All right, all right. You're so right. I don't want to wake her up," she agreed. Still, it was tough, not pushing his tease-buttons, when he looked so adorable. He was trying to bring one of the borrowed baby walkers back to life, which was why he was hunkered down on her peach carpet, surrounded by nuts and bolts and tools. She usually saw him flying around town in his Porsche, or looking like Mr. Drop-Dead-Handsome Doctor at some gathering. And maybe these were images that Justin chose to cultivate, but Winona had still had the feeling that finding a place where he could kick off his boots and just tinker wasn't something Justin got to do often.

The TV was on in the background, but neither was watching the sitcom. They just wanted the chance to click up the volume if any further developments were reported on the Asterland plane emergency landing. Temporarily, though, they might as well have been on an island alone together—except for the sleeping baby.

"So...what'd your boss say about the Angel situation?" Justin asked her.

"Well, deserted and neglected kids generally come under my bailiwick, anyway, so Wayne didn't have to give me permission to handle the problem. It was automatic. He did seem a little startled when I showed up at the station this afternoon with the baby in a front pack. But no one at the station right now has time to worry about anything but the plane crash. Everyone's descended on Royal today, if not in person than through the wires—from state cops to feds, TV and press, the aviation safety folks, diplomats and state people—''

"I know." Justin motioned toward the TV. In the hour they'd had the tube switched on, the local news had interrupted every few minutes to provide an update on the circus. "My Texas Cattleman's group was especially involved with the citizens from both countries. We've offered to help, and I hope the authorities take us up on it. I realize that they have to sweep for evidence and prints and all first...but you can see how much this crisis is driving the town nuts. Everyone wants to know the same thing. What caused that emergency landing? Fine, if it was a mechanical failure, but could it have been terrorists or sabotage?''

"From what I've heard, that specific jet has an outstanding history for being one of the safest planes in the air. And she was deluxe to the nth degree, no expense spared for security or comfort. It's pretty hard to swallow that it was just a plain old mechanical failure—at least if the problem was carelessness." Winona pulled a couch pillow on to her lap, finding it hard to take her eyes off Justin. Last she knew, he'd long reached the multi-millionaire status...which made it all the more fun to watch him bumbling with a screwdriver.

"So what was the buzz at your station house? Your cops find any reason to think there was foul play connected to the emergency landing?''

"There was no evidence leading in that direction this afternoon...but really, it's way too soon to say. They may have collected all the relevant evidence, but it will still take weeks of testing procedures before we have complete answers. The whole world knows how much tension there was between the two countries of Asterland and Obersbourg, though…and that Texas party was the first and only thing that brought those two countries together and talking in more than a decade. I really think you're right, Justin. You and the Texas Cattleman's Club guys should be brought in, both to question and get some advice, and I'll be surprised if you don't get that call.''

''I wasn't as involved as some of the other members. But I still want to help, if there's any chance. And I did know all of the people involved.'' Justin righted the baby walker, pushed it around the carpet. Sighed. And then turned it upside down to work on it again. ''Frightening. To think you could eat dinner with someone, shake their hand, make a joke and laugh with them…and that they could deliberately have had something to do with a near-fatal plane crash.''

''Or that someone could intend harm to so many good people.'' She leaned forward to peer over the edge of the bassinet. She cared about the plane crash. She cared about her job. But at the moment—all day really—only one thing dominated her mind and heart.

''You're not going to wake her up again, are you?''

Winona's jaw dropped. ''Are you out of your mind? I may have only been a mother for a day, but I learned that hours ago. Never wake up a sleeping baby. And if *you* do, I'll have to kill you.''

His chuckle tickled her into a smile, but then he shot her a more serious look. ''So, what's the deal on your squirt there? What's the legal process—what happens to her now?''

''Well, the first thing you already know. An abandoned baby starts out with a medical checkup, no matter how healthy the child appears to be. In this day of AIDS and drug use and all, there's no placing a baby—even temporarily— without knowing the health picture. But that was a piece of cake. She couldn't have gotten a cleaner bill of health.''

''Yeah, so you said this morning. So, then what?''

''Then, normally, she'd be turned over to Social Services,

and they'd find a foster-care arrangement for her.'' Winona's arms tightened around the pillow. ''The court will get more directly involved as soon as something more definitive is established about the parents. And that's my job. Finding the parents. Especially the mom. I have to find out what their story is, and why the baby was abandoned.''

''And how do you go about doing that?''

It seemed odd that she'd never told Justin any details about her job before, but then, there'd never been a reason for this kind of thing to come up in conversation. ''There are lots of ways for me to pick up clues. Now that I have the baby's age pinned down—at least ballpark—I can start checking hospital records, see if I can get a lead into young women having babies at that time. Then I can check the papers, same reason. Check the 911 calls, emergencies, abuse, deaths, anything called in around the time the child was abandoned, to see if there could be any obvious connection.''

''Uh-huh. What else?''

''Then…well, after that, I zoom straight for my at-risk kids. You know how it is in Royal. This is a wealthy community, so on the surface it'd seem we wouldn't have that many kids in trouble. But I keep finding that the very rich and very poor have a lot in common. In both types of families, there are kids raising themselves. Alone a lot of hours. Parents moving near an edge with drugs or alcohol. Divorces, absentee adults. Any way you cut it, it's the lonely kids who tend to sleep around—and look for trouble. So one of the things I always do is run a computer check for runaways.''

''And—?''

''And then I'll check the truancy lists. The arrest lists. Then I'll call the high schools and junior highs for girls with a high absentee record. Talk to the counselors about girls who were pregnant. I started some things in motion this afternoon, but it'd be pretty unusual to land answers overnight. It almost always takes some time.''

"Okay, Win…but what if you don't manage to locate the mother after going through all that?"

She frowned, suddenly aware that she was clenching and unclenching her hands—and that Justin was watching her. "That's not an issue. It's early days yet. Believe me, I'll find the mother. I've done it before."

"But what if you don't?" Justin righted the baby walker again, and this time, it seemed to push along without lurching like a drunken sailor. He set it aside, heaved to his feet and shook his legs as if to shake out the kinks—but his eyes never left her face.

"Well, then, there are other possibilities. A girl in trouble is the most logical choice for the mother. And frankly, I'm about as qualified as anyone in this county to find that kind of girl." For some blasted reason, her fingers were trying to clench into fists again. She folded her arms across her chest, aggravated that she couldn't seem to control the nervous movements. It wasn't like her.

"I know you are, Win." Justin's voice was low, caring. "You know what it's like for a kid to be abandoned. I was never surprised when you aimed to work with juveniles when you decided to be a cop. But you can't possibly find the parents every time there's a problem with a child."

"Well, no, of course not. And as far as Angel…possibly her mother is a married mother with an abusive husband— or that kind of story—which means that she isn't likely to show up on any record. In fact, someone like that can be almost impossible to trace. And another possibility…"

"What?"

"…another possibility is the kind of girl who's kept a pregnancy hidden for nine months. It seems impossible, but we all know that it happens—you've heard those stories surface on the news every once in a while. This one, though, had to do more than just hide the pregnancy, because the baby's already a couple months old. But the problem is the same. There has to be a record of something for us to be able to trace it. And if someone is absolutely determined to keep a pregnancy secret—and has some enablers somehow, someway—we really may never know who the mother is.''

"Okay. So we've covered most of the possible scenarios, good and bad. But in the meantime, what's supposed to happen to our miniature princess here, while you're going through all those record searches and waiting?"

Instinctively her hand shot to her stomach, as if to quell the sudden churning going on in her tummy. Normally she could eat red-hot chili, follow it up with an O.D.-size hot fudge sundae, and never have a digestive problem. But all day, she'd been thinking about what "was supposed to" happen to Angel next…and making herself sick every time she let those fears surface. "Well, the court usually places her in foster care, through Social Services. Like I already told you."

"I know what you told me, Win," Justin said gently. "That's why I'm asking you for the details. So I can understand the situation better."

Again she pressed hard on her stomach, then met his eyes. "Potentially, down the road, she's adoptable. She's a young baby, healthy, and though it's not fair, her being blond and blue-eyed makes her extra desirable in the adoption market. But for that to happen, we have to find the parents—and find that they deliberately abandoned her, really don't want her and will legally sign off. Or we could find that the parents are dead. But otherwise…"

"Yeah. It's that 'otherwise' that happened to you, wasn't it?" Justin had been standing, but now he plunked down on the couch next to her. His gaze prowled her face with the quiet, determined intent of a hunter. "You were in the foster-care system from the time you were six, right? But there was something about how you couldn't be adopted. I remember the families and neighbors talking when the Gerards brought you home. I just don't remember the details."

"There weren't a lot of details. It was pretty cut-and-dried." She glared at him, not in anger, but in self-defense.

At twenty-eight years old, it was about damn time she quit letting this past-history crap bother her. "I wasn't adoptable because my mother was alive and could have come back for me at any time. So I was basically stuck in the foster-care system until I was eighteen."

"You never mentioned your mom before. Or anything about what you remember from when you were real little."

She shrugged, but she could feel an old, aching sense of haunting from the inside out. "My parents' story was older than time. They were two young kids, hot in love—too hot to keep a lid on their hormones. When my mom got pregnant, they both dropped out of school. Two sixteen-year-old idiots with no money and no job skills—undoubtedly thinking they could live on sex and love. The fun part didn't last long. My dad died, some kind of car accident. I have no memory of him at all. But I was with my mom until I was six."

"And that's when she took off."

She shifted restlessly, not meaning to move closer to Justin. She just never liked talking about feelings or the past. "I keep thinking one of these days I could find her. I still run a search every once in a while. But the point is, back then, she couldn't handle me. I certainly didn't realize it then—but I do now. She was in trouble in every way a woman can be in trouble. Alone, broke, a small child to take care of, thinking a little drug here and a little alcohol there would take the edge off the worry, no skills, getting more desperate with every loser she took up with."

Justin fell silent for a moment. "Win...why didn't you ever mention any of this before?"

"Because there's nothing to say. I work with girls like her every day—girls in trouble because they've gotten over their heads, made one mistake and watched the rest of their lives fall down like a stack of dominos. The only thing my mom ever really did wrong was fall in love—or should I say, fall in lust—too young. Cripes, Justin, you know all this—"

He shook his head. "No, actually, I didn't. I remember

my mom talking to my dad. I knew you'd been abandoned when you were a kid. And that your mom had left you with a note, that she'd be back for you as soon as she wasn't so broke, something like that. And I remember the Gerards being furious—''

That made her blink. "The Gerards were furious? About what?"

He lifted a hand. "I was seventeen, Win. I wasn't listening that much to neighborhood stories. But there was some story about when Sissy Gerard first saw you…I don't know what foster family you were with, but it was at a county fair, something like that. Something about the way the family treated you that infuriated her. She came home, told Paget that he was hiring a lawyer and they were getting you away from those people and bringing you home—and that it was going to be your last home until you were grown."

"I didn't know that. I didn't remember any of it, either," Winona admitted. "I just remember the Gerards. Sissy and Paget's faces in this sterile Social Services office. She just wrapped her arms around me as if she'd known me forever. God. They are such good people."

"Yeah, they are." Justin scratched his chin, his eyes suddenly lightening up. "And you were a pistol and a half back then. Clawed anybody who was nice to you. Spit at all the boys. Fought on the playground—"

She had to grin. "Hey, you dog, whose side are you on?"

"Yours. Always yours." His tone turned so quiet that she had to quit chuckling and suddenly looked at him. Really looked. But he was already talking again. "So this baby is going into foster care? In fact, pretty immediately?"

"No." The single syllable was out before she could stop it.

"What's this No? Isn't that what you pretty much told me happens to an abandoned child?"

"The baby has to go somewhere—a place that's honored by Social Services and the court—until something is determined about her parents. Whether they're around and fit, or whatever. And that place is usually foster care. But if the foster-care system is crowded—and right now it's disastrously crowded—then someone else can be assigned temporary guardianship, if they fit the criteria.''

"Win."

"What?"

His voice wasn't a whisper, but melted butter couldn't have been softer. "You don't want to give her up, do you?"

"I don't want her going in foster care. Lost in the foster-care system, like I was." Her own voice came out fierce and sharp. She couldn't seem to help it. "I fell for her the minute I laid eyes on her. I admit it. And I admit that's stupid. A good cop never gets emotionally involved. But whoever left her on my doorstep, Justin, must have known me somehow. It's hard to pretend that doesn't matter. It does, to me. I just want to know that if she goes back to her parents, they're in a position to take good care of her. And until then…''

"You want to keep her."

"I don't want her in foster care," she repeated. A thousand memories were in her head. She didn't have the words for any of them. She only knew that they added up to one thing. She didn't want—she refused to think about—this baby living the childhood she had, flip-flopped between homes and people who neither wanted her nor had room or time for her. But damnation. Somehow, totally unlike her, she could suddenly feel so much emotion welling that her eyes were actually stinging. It was ridiculous. She never lost control like that—not with Justin, never with Justin.

Obviously she had to find an immediate way to lighten things up. She forced a grin—her infamous snappy grin—and cocked an eyebrow at him. Considering all the times he'd joked about marrying her, this should be a guaranteed way to get a laugh out of him. "Normally, the court wouldn't consider a single working woman to be a good bet for that temporary guardianship business. You wouldn't like to marry me, would you? It would really up my chances."

Four

Justin felt his heart stop, then start galloping at breakneck pace.

Winona wasn't *really* asking to marry him. He realized that. Completely. Marriage had become a ritual tease subject between them, because he'd asked her to marry him so many times. She'd always assumed he was joking, so it was perfectly natural that she would joke back with him the same way.

There were just a few tiny differences in these circumstances, though.

He'd always meant those offers.

And the sudden advent of the baby in Winona's life was obviously deeply affecting her. She'd never admitted that she needed help with anything—and for damn sure, she'd never given him the opportunity to come through for her in any way. Justin didn't quite comprehend all the emotional ramifications for her with this baby, but he was dead positive of one thing. He'd been waiting for a chance—any chance—with her for years now. And he wasn't about to let it go.

"Okay, let's do it," he said lightly.

For the first time all evening, the haunted tension left her eyes and she laughed. Really laughed. "Sure. Nothing to it, right? Just get a license and hit the Justice of the Peace. Just what you were dying to do this week."

"Actually, it sounds like a lot of fun to me." He leaned back, as if he could find nothing more important to do than stretch out his long legs.

She was still laughing. "I can just see the headlines in the social column on Sunday. Royal's Most Eligible Bachelor Finally Cuffed By A Cop. And I'm sure there'd be some comments about the bride having to give up her six-year-old Jeep and suffer driving your Porsche—not to mention having to face up to all the trials of suddenly being filthy rich—"

"Shut up, Win. I know you were joking, but why don't you think about it? You sounded really serious to me about wanting to keep this baby."

"I was. I am…but holy mackerel, Justin, I never meant it about getting married. It was just a joke. It wouldn't even solve anything, because Angel's mother could show up at any time. Today, even. Or tomorrow—"

"And maybe she won't ever show. But even if she knocks on your door in a matter of hours, the courts wouldn't just let her have the baby back. Isn't that what you were just explaining? That it's not automatic that the mother would get Angel back—not after abandoning her the way she did." It wasn't hard for Justin to fill in the blanks when Win's fears were right in her eyes giving him easy clues what to say. "So no matter what, Angel is going to be 'housed' somewhere for a while—and that could be a long while. Long enough to make a difference in her life, if she's in a good situation. Or a bad one."

"I know, I know. That's exactly what's driving me crazy." She scraped a hand through her hair, making the curls spring up in tufts. She faced him, her eyes so fierce. Soft-fierce. "I can't stand worrying that she'd be put in a bad place for her. All I really want is to be able to take care of her until we know for sure what's what in her life. I *know* that I'll love her. And that almost anything's better than being thrown into the limbo of foster care. The overcrowding. The never knowing how long you can stay in one place or another. I can't stand it. I know that's irrational and emotional and stupid, but I've *been* there, Justin. And I hate it that that could happen to Angel, to this baby. I know it's nuts, I—''

"Win, I don't really give a damn if it's nuts or not. If I understood what you told me earlier, they'd consider you for temporary guardian, if you were married. Is that true or not true?''

"True. Actually, it's true that they would consider me anyway—but I'd almost certainly get turned down right now. I don't know of any circumstances where a single woman's been allowed to foster. Not here. It's always a two-parent family—''

"So let's get married.''

She tried to answer and ended up sputtering on another bubble of laughter. She laughed harder. Then quit. Then hiccuped.

He'd never seen Winona undone before. Had no idea she could be—at least by him.

When he lifted a hand, he knew he intended to kiss her. When his fingers touched her cheek, pushed back, so gently, into her hair, cupping her head toward him…he knew what he was doing then, too. Sort of. He sure as hell knew how to kiss a woman.

But he'd never kissed Winona before. Any kind of kiss. Any way. Possibly because he'd known that even one small kiss was never going to be simple. Not with her. Not for him.

She wasn't expecting the kiss, because her forehead puckered in a frown and her eyes widened in surprise and confusion when he kept coming closer. But when his fingers laced in her hair, she didn't move. When his mouth honed in on hers, she didn't pull away. She went as still as a statue.

But nothing about Win resembled a cold statue. She tasted fragile. Soft. Warm. Alluring.

She made a small sound when his mouth touched hers, tasted, came back for more. Win rarely wore perfumes, yet he suddenly felt surrounded by her scents. Her tongue still carried the echo of the vanilla cappuccino he'd made her. Her hair was a tumble of springy, unruly curls, threaded with that hint of strawberry shampoo she used. And she was always slathering cream on her face and hands because her skin was so dry, and that was the other scent. Almonds. Vanilla. Strawberry. All edible stuff.

Like her.

She made another sound, and her fingers suddenly clutched his arm, as if to push him away. Only she didn't push him away, and beneath his mouth, her lips were suddenly moving, trembling like a whisper, her eyelashes swooshing down as if the light in the room were suddenly too bright. The TV flashed on a news interruption, which technically they'd both been rabidly interested in earlier. Now, he didn't look up, and neither did she.

Those first exploring kisses turned deeper, silkier, sexier. The fingers clutching his arm suddenly wound, tight and hard, around his neck. Tongues tangled, tangoed. He kissed and kept on kissing, but now he could feel her skin heating, feel her body yielding, bowing to his on an angry groan of a sigh. He heard the anger in that groan, and a thousand years from now—when he had time—he'd want to smile. Win had had no idea she'd feel desire with him.

Neither had he. He'd been pretty sure, for years now, that his panting after her had all been one-sided. Yeah, there was a kind of love. The way you could love a brother at the same time you smacked him upside the head. The way you loved an old friend who knew your childhood secrets. It was good love. All love was good love. But it wasn't man-woman love.

It wasn't heat like a volcano, and a hurricane rush, and wanting that could claw you from the inside out, if you let it.

He wanted to let it. He wanted to peel that big sweatshirt off her and bow her back into the couch cushions, into the shadows, and dunk her in sensuality so deep, so hot, that neither of them could get up until it was over. He wanted to see her naked. To touch her naked. To have her naked.

But there was a sleeping baby only three feet away. And these few potent kisses were suddenly raising questions that Justin never thought he'd get the chance to ask. Fire or no fire, need or no need, he was afraid of losing the answers he wanted if he moved too fast.

So he eased up on that last kiss. Tried to remember how to breathe normally. Smoothed his hand back up above her neck. Pressed his forehead to her forehead, eyes closed, loving how she was huffing like a freight train, too.

And that helped him relax. And smile. "Hey, Win...I'm richer than Croesus. You did know that, didn't you?"

Her eyes were still more liquid than a lake, but she gave him a short frown, expressing confusion. "Am I supposed to care about that?"

"Yeah. Because it matters. It matters because I can put a marriage together faster than most people. And get those temporary guardian papers going through the legal system. You want this baby? We can make it happen."

"Justin..." She swallowed, hard, when he lurched to his feet.

He'd already heard the baby stir. He pushed into shoes, glanced around for his jacket, but then he met her eyes again. Those soft, liquid-as-a-lake-blue eyes. Liquid for him. For the first time in all these years, liquid for him. "I don't know about you and me. But we've known each other forever, Winona. And again, I've got the money, the resources to put this together fast. The resources to make it easy for both of us—to get in, to get out, to do whatever we both want to do. There's no woman in my wings. Is there a man in yours?''

She blinked. ''No.''

''Come on. I need you to be frank with me. There has to be some guy—''

''No.''

Well, hell. He couldn't hold back a grin. He ruffled her curls, grabbed his jacket and let himself out. And yeah, he'd left the proposal hanging between them. But there was no way Winona Raye would ever—in this life—give him a yes on the spur of the wild moment like that.

By his leaving right then, he'd given her no chance to say no.

That wasn't just progress. As far as Justin was concerned, it was damn close to manna from heaven.

Snuggling the baby more securely on her shoulder, Winona paced the house from window to window. Justin's satin-black Porsche had disappeared from her driveway an hour ago, but she kept looking out anyway. Maybe his visit had been a mirage. Or maybe he'd put a drug in her coffee—because something had dropped her off in Oz for a few hours, for darn sure.

Angel let out a sleepy burp, making Winona smile. Still, she kept on pacing and patting, pacing and patting. Really, her brief sojourn into Oz was downright funny. She'd actually imagined Justin seriously asking her to marry him. Not joking this time. But low-down serious.

Boy, was that funny.

So funny that even after the baby fell asleep big time—for the night, she hoped—Winona still couldn't think, couldn't breathe, couldn't sleep. She was as tired as a worn-out hound, yet still pacing the floors in the dark.

He'd asked if there was a man in her life. And simply couldn't seem to credit her avowal that there wasn't.

At midnight, she prowled to the refrigerator for some

milk—poured out a half a cup, all she had in the house—
and carted it back to her bedroom. She climbed in between
the cobalt-blue sheets and mounded the pillows behind her
head, sipping, staring out the windows at a lover's moon and
a sky full of stars.

There'd been men. But not in a while. Once she'd realized
that she'd been the one screwing up the relationships, she'd
backed off from trying. She wasn't any good at getting
close—not in the sack or out of it. Sex wasn't the only problem, but it was a nuisance of a big one. She had no objections
to intimacy, getting naked, big inhibitions, nothing like that.

She'd just figured, a long time back, that her sweat with
intimacy was about abandonment. Being abandoned once in
a lifetime was enough. If you had your soul ripped out once,
most sane people didn't volunteer for a repeat experience.
But when that translated into a relationship…well. She could
lie there beneath a guy. Smile. Make the right movements.
Make the right groans.

In fact, she had.

Frankly, she thought she was pretty good—if not downright outstanding—at faking it. But there didn't seem much
point. She wasn't that unhappy alone. She liked her job, her
life. She had friends, respect in the community. She *liked*
feeling contained. Safe. So maybe she had a hard time trusting others at a gut level. So what?

But she hadn't liked that kiss from Justin. Her lips still felt
bee-stung, her nerves sharp-stung even more. She didn't let
go like that. Ever. She never went loopy, dizzy, spinning high
with any man—and certainly not for a few ridiculous idiot
kisses.

What the Sam Hill did Justin think he was *doing?* Kissing
her? Offering to marry her?

Something was wrong with him, she concluded. Bad
wrong. Seriously wrong. The idea soothed her. She set down
the empty milk cup and curled up under the covers, immediately starting to relax. She simply should have thought this

through earlier. If Justin was acting bananas, there had to be a reason for it. Whatever it was, she'd talk to him. Help him. Like the friends they were.

And she'd reassure him, of course, that she realized he'd never meant that offer of marriage.

Two mornings later, as Justin drove to the site of the Asterland plane crash landing, his mind was on Winona, not business. Weddings, not plane crashes. Love, not problems. But the closer he got to the scene of the accident, the faster his mood turned grave.

As of hours after the crash landing, the sheriff had set up a roadblock, both to protect the evidence and to discourage strangers and gawkers. The cop immediately recognized Justin's black Porsche, though, and waved him on.

The road ran out within yards, and turned into a desertlike hard pan surface. After spring rains, possibly the land was more forgiving, even decent grazing ground, but right now it definitely wasn't the most hospitable spot in Texas. Most vehicles could undoubtedly traverse the hard surface, but with his baby, Justin had to slow to a crawl. Finally, the plane loomed in sight. And when Justin finally stopped the car and climbed out, a witch-bitter wind bit his cheeks and stung his eyes.

"Justin!"

He'd already recognized the other two members of the Texas Cattleman's Club—and their practical, sturdier vehicles—but for a second, the look of the private jet had stunned him into staring. At the sound of his name, though, he promptly pivoted and hiked toward his friends. Typically, Dakota Lewis didn't seem to notice that the January morning was mean-freezing; his jacket was gaping open. At least Matthew Walker had a red nose and cheeks like his own.

"I'm sorry to be late," he grumped. "I started out early enough, but the Porsche does what the Porsche wants to do.

One of these days, I'm going to turn into a grown-up and get a serious car.''

"We've only been waiting a few minutes," Dakota assured him.

Again, Justin looked around. "Hell. If this isn't enough to put chills up your spine."

Just like the others, he'd hightailed it to exactly this site when the plane had first gone down, but it wasn't dark now; there were no flames, no crying passengers…there was no sound at all but the shriek of a winter wind. Acres of Texas flatland stretched in all directions, bleached of all color and life at this time of year, and in the middle of that ice-gray desert was the mirror-silver of the plane, just sitting there. She was listing a bit, but she didn't look as if she'd crashed or had an emergency landing. She just looked like an alien vehicle in the middle of a Star Trek episode. Big. Silent. A scream of high technology in a land of rattlesnakes and coyotes. And the door to the small jet gaped open like a mouth waiting for a dentist's probe.

"I'm still surprised that the cops called us." Matthew brought up the rear as they all strode toward the metal plane stairs.

"I don't believe it was the cops' idea that we were called in. I suspect it was Princess Anna's family. No one in Asterland or Obersbourg has any real contacts in America except for the Texas Cattleman's Club, so I think it's pretty natural they'd want us as part of the investigation. They know us. They trust us." Dakota led the way inside the plane. "It'd be different if some clues had surfaced as to the cause of the emergency landing. Of course, a fire's the best way in hell to destroy evidence. But right now, I think everyone's still worried about sabotage. If some answers don't surface real soon, I'd be surprised if Asterland doesn't send over its own team of investigators."

"Well, I hear you, but you're retired from the Air Force," Matthew said to Dakota. "If anyone belongs here, you do.

God knows, I'm willing to help, but I can't imagine anything I can really do."

"Same here," Justin said. "But I think the point is to get a fresh pair of eyes on the site. Experts have already been over the place with a fine-tooth comb, but we're the only ones who knew all the people on board. I think they're hoping we'll find something that no one else had any reason to notice." He frowned. "But I thought Aaron and Ben were going to join us?"

Dakota nodded. "Ben is. In fact, he should be here shortly. He cell-phoned a few minutes ago just to let us know he'd been tied up. Not Aaron, though—Aaron took off for Washington a couple days ago and he isn't back yet."

"He went to Washington? Related to this problem?" Matthew asked.

Dakota shook his head. "I don't really know what Aaron's doing there, but when he was home over the holidays, I knew there was some problem with his job. I understood that he'd taken a leave of absence from his diplomatic work, so I figure he's at the embassy in Washington—but all I really know was that he was really unhappy and worried about something."

"I had the same impression," Justin agreed. "In fact, I tried to talk to him at our Texas Cattleman's Club shindig." But then he'd gotten caught up watching Winona dance. Watching Win smile. Watching Win breathe. And that fast, she stole into his mind all over again. Memories snapped into his mind, of her holding the baby, and then of her holding...him. Kissing him. Coming alive in his arms in a way he'd never believed could happen.

The plane-crash scene, though, slapped him back to reality. And Matthew was still talking about Aaron Black.

"I tried to talk to him the night of the party, too, but then he got dancing with that plain-faced teacher with the sweet smile. What's her name? Pamela?"

"Pamela Miles," Justin affirmed. He remembered her, not

from the night of the party so much, but from treating her the morning after the plane's emergency landing. "She was on this plane flight, in fact. Headed to be an exchange teacher in Asterland—at least before the crash."

"Well, she sure didn't have her mind on teaching that night. I'd never guess that Aaron would go for that kind of gal, but they were sure glued closer than peanut butter and jelly for a while there. Anyway, I never got a chance to ask him anything about his job. He left early the night of the party. And in the meantime..."

In the meantime, all three of them fell abruptly silent as they slowly walked through the plane. Justin glanced at the other two men, but the view seemed to disturb all of them the same way. The whole group had been here the morning of the crash landing. Justin remembered it well. He'd gotten the phone call, driven here like a bat out of hell, saw the smoke billowing out, hurled out of his car and started working. He'd been a doctor that morning. Nothing else. Trauma medicine used to be his adrenaline flow, his heartbeat.

It wasn't anymore.

He couldn't let it be.

But the morning of the crash, for damn sure, all he'd seen were the passengers, their injuries, their frightened faces. Now the silence was eerie and the devastation inside the plane as frightening as a bomb site.

"Hell. What a mess," Matthew muttered.

"It could have been worse."

"A ton worse." Dakota's gaze riveted on the cockpit, with which he was obviously more familiar than either of the others. "You saw more of this than any of us, Justin."

"Because I was inside right after the crash? Yeah, I suppose. But I only saw people. Patients. It's all I was looking for or looking at. I never gave a second look to anything about the plane."

"Well, let me fill you both in on what I know. This is where the fire started..." Dakota motioned, and then motioned again, "Robert Klimt was sitting here. And Lady Helena across the aisle there. Not surprisingly, those two were hurt worse than anyone else on the flight."

The three of them had a passenger list and a diagram showing where each person had been seated, but Justin couldn't keep his eyes off the plane's interior. The overhead compartments were all yawning open, debris spilled all over the aisles and seats. No one had been allowed to recover their personal belongings yet. The fire had left a gaping hole with black char climbing the walls and the carpet still seeping and stinking from the water and extinguisher chemicals.

"As bad as it is, it's still like looking at a miracle," Matthew said soberly. "I don't know how anyone walked away from this. It's too damn easy to imagine everyone being killed, the whole thing up in flames."

"Yeah. If this was the act of a terrorist, I hope to hell we get him. And soon."

For a moment Justin couldn't speak. His fingertips went ice cold, the way they did when he woke up from nightmares sometimes, memories of Bosnia still moaning through his mind. This kind of crisis was exactly why he'd accepted the Texas Cattleman's Club's invitation to join their group. Maybe outsiders thought they were a male bastion social club, but Justin knew how committed the men were to saving innocents. Too damn often, neither the law nor any government could protect innocents. Not in any country.

He sucked in a breath, forcing those old nightmare memories to fade. At least there'd been no small children involved in this plane flight.

His gaze swept and reswept the plane's interior. He saw an overturned romance paperback on the floor. A woman's red high-heel shoe lying on its side. A black driving glove. A small carry-on had upended, revealing a spill of lingerie that looked like a bride's trousseau—Matthew muttered something about Jamie Morris and what he'd heard about her marriage to some higher-up dignitary in Asterland's government. Down the aisle a little farther was a snakeskin purse, also lying open, with lipsticks and combs and what all strewn down the aisle. There was a sweater here, a coat there. The acrid after-smell of burned plastic and chemicals.

The door to the pilot's cabin stood ajar, the cold morning sun streaming through the windows. It seemed crazy to notice the dust spinning in the sunlight, as if anything about this scene were remotely normal.

But then a sharp, bright glint caught his attention. On the carpet, near where Lady Helena had been sitting on the flight, Justin hunkered down, frowning.

"Matt. Dakota."

"What?" Matthew bent down, too, but Justin raised a cautious hand to prevent him from touching anything.

Dakota pushed closer, sensing from the sudden excitement and seriousness of the other two that they'd found something important. He looked over Justin's shoulders. "That *can't* be what I think it is," he breathed.

The two stones were just lying in the carpet, not noticeably separable from all the other debris. A handkerchief wasn't far. The black driving glove. Ash and messes from the fire. But the two stones were a startling contrast to everything else.

One was a black harlequin opal.

The other, a three-carat emerald.

Justin exchanged glances with Dakota and Matthew. Matt's face had bleached white. Probably his own had, too.

None of the men could give a holy hoot about gems—but all of them recognized these two stones. The jewels were too rare and distinctive to be mistaken for anything else, even by lay people such as them.

The whole town knew the legend of the Texas Cattleman's Club's three jewels. And Justin distinctly remembered the old story being retold at the last Texas Cattleman's Club party—Riley Monroe recounting the old yarn to one of the Asterlanders. The townspeople never seemed to get tired of the jewel tale, even if they never believed it was true. It just didn't matter. It was a great story, and specifically a story with a message about the values of leadership, justice and peace—the Club's motto.

Two of the stones in the old legend, of course, were a black harlequin opal and a great big green emerald.

Just like these two.

Amazingly like these two.

Exactly like these two.

Matthew wildly shook his head. "I don't get this. Someone tried to steal our stones? But I didn't think anyone really believed they existed—much less that anyone had a clue where we had them locked up all these years."

"Neither did I. In fact, none of this makes any sense. If there'd been a break-in at night, Riley Monroe would have immediately contacted one of us. And obviously nothing happened during the day, when people are around, or we'd have easily known about that, too." Justin was already lurching to his feet. So was Dakota. "But the frightening thing is…if those two gems *were* stolen—then where is our red diamond?"

All three men swore at the same time, even as they were pawing and prowling around the plane, searching every nook and cranny and sifting through all the debris. All three stones were priceless, but the red diamond was so rare it was literally beyond price, beyond even a collector's dreams. "It doesn't make sense that anyone would have taken the other two stones and left the diamond," Dakota grumped.

"It doesn't make sense that any of them could have been stolen to begin with," Justin shot back, and then sucked in a swear word.

"What?" Dakota demanded. "Did you find it? The red diamond?"

No, he hadn't found the stone. He'd found a creased sheet of paper that would never have drawn his eye if the word *emerald* hadn't been written on it in a big, slashing scrawl

Frowning, he noted the Asterland stationery. "I don't know what this is," Justin told the others. "It's not a letter. It doesn't seem to be written to anyone specific—at least there's no name on the stationery. But someone jotted down the town legend about the jewels. The whole history. The Texas soldier who found the stones on a fallen comrade in the War with Mexico, took the stones home to Royal, then made it rich on oil before there was any reason to spend them...."

"What else?" Matthew couldn't see at the same time as the other two men.

"The whole thing about the jewels. That red diamonds were traditionally called the stone of kings because they stood for leadership. There's a scrawled history of black opals here, specifically black harlequin opals, and how, symbolically, they were credited as being healing gems as well as allowing their owners to 'bring justice' to those around them. And the emerald is described as a symbol of peace and peacemakers." Justin looked up.

"Leadership, justice, peace," Dakota echoed. Again, the men exchanged quiet glances. They all knew why those words had been chosen as the Texas Cattleman's Club motto—and what each man had vowed to protect when he'd been asked to become part of the group.

"I still don't understand any of this," Matthew said irritably. "The whole world knows about the legend. But who could possibly have known that the stones were real, much less know where we had the jewels locked up? Where's the damn red diamond? And...for God's sake...do you two think the jewel theft had anything to do with the crash landing of this plane?"

Justin lifted a hand helplessly. "I don't know how it could. But the coincidence is pretty hard to ignore."

Dakota said swiftly, "We need to get together—as soon as we can get hold of Aaron and Ben. But even sooner than that, at least one of us needs to get to the Club. Find out if the red diamond is still there. Talk to Riley Monroe. And find out what happened to our safe.''

Justin pushed a hand through his hair. ''I'll volunteer to do anything you want…but to be honest, I'll have a hard time meeting until later tonight—say, eight o'clock, earliest. I have patients back-to-back until then. I realize how critical this is, and I *can* cancel patients if I have to, but—''

''No, it's all right, Justin. I'd rather wait until after dinner tonight, too,'' Matt concurred. ''We've got a better chance of Ben joining us. And if Aaron isn't back, we could at least have consulted with him by phone before then. Because of his diplomatic connections and knowledge, I really think Aaron should be brought into this before we make any decisions.''

''Yeah. Agree.'' Dakota nodded. ''But I'll hit the Club this afternoon—or as fast as I can. I have to cancel a meeting to get freed up—but I'll try, because I think we'll all go nuts worrying whether the red diamond's been stolen until we know for sure. But as far as a meeting time for all of us to get together, I agree with you, too. Let's aim for tonight. Justin?''

He'd already turned toward the plane door, as the other two had. ''You want to take the emerald and the opal back with you?'' Justin asked, assuming that was why Dakota had signaled him out.

''No. Hell. If the safe's been broken into, we all need to decide together what to do with these two stones for security in the meantime. But you hold them until then. No, that wasn't the issue. I was going to suggest that you be careful what you say to Winona Raye.''

Justin's expression had to reveal his astonishment. ''Why on earth would you think I'd be seeing Winona?''

''Because we all saw the way you were looking at her at the party.'' Dakota slapped him on the back, then hiked past him. So did Matt. ''Far as I'm concerned, you couldn't get involved with a better lady. I think the world of her. Far as

I know, so does this whole town. So mostly I was just trying to get a rise out of you—but it does keep occurring to me that this situation is getting seriously complicated. Right now, the police don't know about the jewels or the theft—much less that there could be any connection to the problem with the Asterland plane. Maybe that information has to come out? There may be no choice.''

Justin nodded. ''But we all know what's at stake—the reason we've guarded our privacy all these years.'' The Club members could hardly have taken off on their private causes across the world if their comings and goings were regular headline news.

''Hell, doc, I'd trust you with my life. You already know that. For that matter, I couldn't think more of Winona. It just crossed my mind that we could be putting her on the spot if she knew something that was being kept from the local cops. At least until we know more facts about the jewel theft and decided what we need to do.''

Justin had no trouble agreeing. The three split up swiftly. Everyone had their own lives and work to attend to. But as Justin headed for his car, the wind whipping a burn on his cheeks, his plan to see Winona for an early dinner went on a front burner.

He'd left her alone for two days now—except for phone calls—to consider marrying him. He'd known she needed time to think. More than likely, she'd had enough time to have a cow and a half over his proposal.

He never intended to put her on the spot about the jewels. He only wanted to put her on the spot about a relationship between them. And nothing as annoying as some priceless stolen jewels was going to keep him from her. Not today. He'd waited as long as he could stand.

Five

"**W**inona!"

Winona had barely pushed open the door to the Royal Diner before the waitress shrieked her name. Sheila abandoned her customer and bustled straight toward her.

"I been hearing all over town about you and that baby! Let's have a look!" Although it was barely the dinner hour, the diner was already filling up. This was not a crowd worried about eating at a fashionably late hour—more likely they were worried about how fast they could get the kids home to bed. Sheila popped her favorite Juicy Fruit gum as she herded Winona and the baby carrier toward a booth in the back, talking the whole while—loud enough, of course, for the whole town to hear.

"Dr. Webb called. Said to put you in a spot away from the drafts and get you started, he'd be here, but he got held up with a patient for a little bit. So you're seeing Dr. Webb, huh? God, he's such a hunk. Could make a girl think about getting a breast reduction just to get his hands on her...but

I guess that's a little tasteless, huh? If you're seeing him and all. But you don't have to worry about me, honey, he'd never look my way…and I can't wait to hear the whole story about that baby. Let's see her, let's see her…well, aren't you a beauty, darlin'.''

Sheila tugged down her waitress uniform, which tended to ride up her thighs with every other step. Years ago, Winona had realized that buying another size uniform wasn't a possibility—not for Sheila. She'd been fighting to stay in a size twelve for half a decade now, and there was no way she was going to let a fourteen win. But right then, she peeled back Angel's blanket and picked up the baby with a long refrain of oohs and aahs.

Because the baby chortled happily for the attention, Winona decided to let Sheila live. Actually, she was too tired to kill her and too old to feel embarrassed at the waitress's loud personal gossip. Still, she pushed off her jacket and sank onto the booth seat, wishing for a long, tall whiskey instead of straight water—and she didn't drink. The thing was, over the last two days, Sheila wasn't the only townsperson who'd made wild, presumptuous assumptions about Winona's relationship with Justin.

It didn't make sense. Folks should have been gossiping ten for a dozen about the plane crash. That was the crisis in town. That was the big news. Who Winona happened to be seeing—or not seeing—shouldn't have mattered to a soul.

And the really crazy thing was that she wasn't even seeing Justin. At least not exactly. Yeah, he'd offered to marry her…and for damn sure, that was why she'd insisted on seeing him right now, today, over dinner, and specifically chosen this public place for the occasion…but there was still no reason from here to Austin that anyone should leap to the conclusion that she was "seeing him." Heaven knew he'd proposed to her fifty times before this. And most folks in Royal had seen her slug him probably that many times—or more.

"Well, okay, honey, if you want to keep it quiet, I won't tell a soul," Sheila boomed, as she settled the baby back in the carrier. "But I hope you realize that no one's curiosity is intended in a mean way. We all love you. We all know you. Anyone who's had a kid in trouble, for years you were the one who stepped in. This here baby, though..." Efficiently she slapped down two paper place mats that read: The Royal Diner—Food Fit For a King! and then extracted her pen and pad from her front hip pocket. "She doesn't look Spanish or Indian or Mexican. Not with that blond hair and blue eyes...but you haven't found the mama yet?"

"Not yet."

Sheila motioned with her pen. "So, what'll you have? Dr. Webb, remember, he said for you to order."

"Really, I'd rather wait for him—"

"No, no. He said you'd be tired from working and from carting the baby around all day. He'll be here. Just ten minutes late, he said. But he wanted you to start eating. Manny—" she motioned toward the grill cook in back "—he says the pork chops are extra tender today."

"I was thinking a salad—"

"Now, you can't build up your strength on leaves and rabbit food, honey. Much less can you build up a bust, and men do tend to like a substantial woman, you know. Did you see my pies up front?" She motioned toward the revolving pie stand near the front door. "Strawberry rhubarb today. And I got a banana cream to die for. You need me to warm up a bottle for the baby? You sleeping with Dr. Webb?"

"Cobb salad. No dessert. Yes, thank you on the bottle, I have one in the diaper bag here. And none of your business."

Sheila cocked up an eyebrow. "Now, hon, with the Gerards gallivanting on vacation the winter months, who'all's gonna give you advice if your friends in town don't? But I don't see the question made you blush, so I'm thinking, no, not yet. Ask me, I'd nail that man fast and any way I could. There's some men you can string along, they like the hunt and chase. But him, I wouldn't risk nothing like that. Too many girls got their eyes on him. He's too cute and too rich. You get a chance, you get that boy in the sack and you don't give him a chance to even look at anyone else.''

"Thank you so much." Winona swiped a hand over her eyes. "Is there anything else you want to offer me advice on? Deodorants? Hemorrhoids? Constipation?''

"There now. You won't be so crabby after you have some food. I'll bring you the chops and my cheddar cheese mashed potatoes. Trust me. You'll like them. And the whole town's been asking whether Wayne's gonna actually let you bring that baby to work right in the police station.''

"It's only a temporary circumstance, my having the baby. It's worked out for a few days. But obviously, I wouldn't have the baby around any situation that could be dangerous. It just takes time to find an answer for—''

"Yeah, yeah." Sheila waved off the politically correct answer. If she couldn't have dirt, she didn't want anything. "So, did you tell the Gerards about the baby yet?''

Winona sighed. To a point, it was easier to answer the questions than exert all the energy it took to duck them. "Yes. They're still vacationing in Japan and having an outstanding time. But I talked to them on the phone two nights ago.''

"They love you." Sheila set out the silverware, working around the baby's carrier in the middle of the table. Two other customers waved hands to get her attention, but she clearly didn't want to move quite yet. "And I just know they'd be happy if you were involved with Justin, because the Webb and the Gerard families were always so close. And really, at your age, hon, I think they'd expect you to be, how should I say it, physically involved—''

Winona propped her chin on her knuckled hand. "Okay. I give up trying to deny it. I'm having wild, unprincipled sex with Dr. Webb. If it'll make y'all happy, tell the town, tell the whole universe—''

She was stunned into immediate silence when she suddenly saw another face appear behind the waitress's—and Justin was grinning to beat the band.

"Now, darlin'. Please don't be giving all the wild details of our sex life to Sheila. You didn't tell her what we did two nights ago in the Porsche, did you?"

Smoothly, as if they'd been a couple for a hundred years, he bent down, bussed the top of her head, chucked the baby's chin, and then plunked down on the opposite side of the booth. "Sheila, I've only got forty minutes, max. I want the greasiest hamburger you've got back there, heavy on the barbecue, and a ton of fries—"

"Like you need to tell me this, sweetheart?" Sheila whirled around, clearly delighted with him, and sashayed off to deliver their order.

Winona needed a second to recover her equilibrium. Five minutes ago, she'd had no equilibrium problems, but suddenly her heart was flopping in her chest louder than a beached whale and her nerves were suffering hiccups. She didn't have nerves. She'd certainly never suffered from arrhythmia—at least until Justin walked in. And that kiss from two nights ago seeped back into her mind with a twinge of guilt.

She felt his gaze on her face. Nothing new, their looking at each other. They'd known each other for five million years, for Pete's sake. Only, nothing was the same since that kiss. He'd never—never—looked at her this way before. As if she were a woman, instead of an old ragtail-younger-neighbor friend. As if she were a woman who sexually interested him. As if he didn't have all that much trouble imagining her in bed. And was enjoying that imagining.

Her gaze frittered around the diner. The red barstools were all taken, the long Formica counter filled up with locals. Booths lined the walls, mostly spilling over with young families, but, traditionally, medical personnel popped over here to grab the counter seats because the hospital was so close by. No one in the medical field ever seemed to eat healthily. On the jukebox, someone was wailing about losing somebody. There was a truck and a cup of a coffee and a dog in the song, so no question it was a country-style wail. Manny, the cook, was visible from the open window of the grill kitchen. He was wearing his beefcake-style white undershirt that showed off his shoulder and upper arm muscles, and he was wielding a black spatula. Sheila patted his butt every time she went by.

The diner was familiar. Comfortable. The teasing was a pain in the keester, but what could Winona expect from a small town where everyone knew her, and, damnation, everybody cared? Hell, she cared, too, and could pry with the best of them when she was in the mood. Normally it was as easy to be in the Royal Diner as at home.

Except tonight.

She felt a sensation of panic, as if her whole world were shifting on her. It wasn't exactly that she *minded* his looking at her in that new way. That intimate, hot, unnerving-damnhim way. But she'd always known what to say to Justin, how to behave, what to do around him, and suddenly all that comfort level was lost.

Finally he got around to saying something. "You look tired, Win."

"Thanks, Doc. That's just what a girl wants to hear."

"And not just a little tired. You look just plain whipped."

Immediately she bristled. What had happened to all the sweet talk he'd used when Sheila'd been around? "Are you looking for a sock right in the *labonza?* I'm not the least tired," she snapped.

The insult went right over his head. "What's wrong?"

Her shoulders sank. The feeling of strangeness disappeared. This was, after all, Justin, who she'd known forever—and who already knew all about Angel. "Everything."

"So. We'll fix this 'everything.' But that's a little tough to do unless you're willing to be a little more specific."

Out it poured. All the frustrations from the last time she'd seen him. Even though technically Angel should have been promptly turned over to Social Services, no one really had a sweat with her temporarily baby-sitting. Still, the whole world, and especially her boss, kept reminding her that the baby showing up on her doorstep didn't mean she had any dibs—or legal rights—on Angel. And she *knew* that. But for the same reason, one of the first things she'd done was check out what was going on with foster care.

"Okay." When Sheila served dinner, Justin didn't even look up, just kept his eyes on hers, encouraging her to keep talking.

"There's no great foster-care family waiting in the wings. The court finds a place when it has to. That's the way it is. So there are the Barkers, who've already taken in two kids, even though they barely had room for the second one. They can take in a baby for a couple of weeks if there's no other place. They're good people, but they don't *want* Angel, Doc."

"Okay."

"And there's another family on the foster-care list...." She pushed her fork around fretfully. "On paper, they're qualified. In reality, we've never put a child with them. He...smells. She dresses vintage Victorian to scrub her bathroom. I'm not saying anything's that terrible, but there seem to be some raisins missing in their bran, you know? They claim to desperately want kids, that they can't have their own, be happy to foster. But I'm telling you—"

"Angel isn't going there." Justin, God love him, didn't waste time phrasing the comment as a question.

Again, her shoulders eased. He understood. "I realize that doesn't mean that I'm the best choice to take care of the baby. Or that I'm entitled. In any way. But—"

"Oh, shut up, Win. You don't have to justify anything to me." He peeked at the snoozing baby as he started wolfing his burger. "So keep on talking. What's happened so far with the parent search? I take it you haven't found the baby's mother?"

"God knows, I'm trying."

"But…?"

She started filling him in. Leading her mom-suspect list were a couple of teenage girls. Both troubled. Both had histories of drinking and truancy. Both came from rich families where the parents had recently shipped them off to residential ranches. "You know the kind of place I'm talking about. They have a dry-out program, but it's also a live-in school, all the academics. The idea is to remove the kids from the environment that was contributing to their trouble, see if professionals and positive peers can't help turn the kids around."

"Actually, I don't know anything about those places, but it's obvious you do."

"Yeah. And some of them are excellent. Kids *do* take a wrong turn sometimes. Especially if they can't get away from bad peer influences on their own. The only thing that ticks me off is how expensive they are, it's not like everyone can take advantage. But, anyway, on those two specific girls— neither of them was pregnant, according to their parents."

"Which means…?"

"Which means nothing. The parents could be lying, thinking that they're protecting their daughters. So I can't be sure until I've checked that out, and that's going to take longer than overnight." She lifted a forkful of cheddar cheese mashed potatoes, but then let it drop again. "In the meantime, I picked up news about another kid. Parents live in a trailer park, dad works in the oil fields, girl got pregnant at fourteen, supposedly had the baby in the family trailer and it died. Only maybe the baby didn't die. Maybe that's what the girl said to avoid trouble, and if so, and if her child was Angel, then it could well have fetal alcohol syndrome—at best. But right now, I have no grounds to haul in the girl and force her to take a medical exam." She glared at Justin. "I'm almost positive that this girl isn't Angel's mother. But if she were…then either of those foster-care families would be the worst place to put a baby with those kinds of special problems.''

"I hear you. You're saying you'd want to take in Angel even more if you thought she had special problems. Not less. But in the meantime, how come you're so positive that that one girl isn't Angel's mom?''

"Well, I can't be *positive*—but whoever is the mom of that baby knew me personally. She had to. I mean, she not only left the baby at my house, but left a personal note to me. And I didn't know that kid in the trailer park from Adam—or anyone in her family.'' Sheila stopped by the table, delivered the warmed bottle and two gigantic pieces of pie, but when she couldn't get another conversation going, moved on again. "I spent hours in the schools today. And on the computer. Found three runaways. Six truant cases. I'm still trying to follow up on all of them. Then I hit the docs, the clinics, the obstetricians, Planned Parenthood. I swear I could smack 'em all upside the head. None of those people talk. They'd guard the confidentiality of a kid in trouble no matter what. It's like trying to get blood out of a turnip. So then I tried calling ministers and priests and rabbi Rachel—''

He glanced over at her plate, and stole some of the chops she wasn't eating.

"They've all got worry-lists of girls or kids they think are promiscuous. But whether any of those girls were for sure pregnant at the time Angel's mom had to be—no one knows. One minister gave me a couple of names to check out. So did one of the vice principals at the high school.''

"But…?'' He held out a tidbit of pork chop on a fork, until she bit into it and chewed.

"But it could be an adult woman. It's not like the mother *had* to be a teenager.'' She swallowed, only to have the exasperating man nudge another bite toward her mouth. "So I called the women's shelter. Asked if anyone was pregnant at the time Angel's mom had to be. Since this woman knew my name, I keep thinking that if I could just get some clues, some ideas, I might recognize her in some way. And I'm looking for a grown-up now, a woman with the means to hide a pregnancy, but for some reason feels she can't keep her baby. Unfortunately, the people at the shelter were as bad as the doctors. Angel's mom could have been right there, but no one was about to tell me. I understand confidentiality. I believe in it, for Pete's sake. Only it's been days now, and I can't get a solid lead to save my life.''

"Win," Justin stopped trying to coax her into more food. "Are you positive that you want a lead?"

The question startled her. "Are you asking me if I'd drag my feet because of wanting the baby for myself?" She shook her head, fast, fiercely. "I admit I've fallen in love with her. I know it's only been three days, but I swear she already feels like she's mine. But there's only one way I can make this right, Justin. To find the mom. To know what the whole story is. Then to legally go after doing whatever's right for Angel. I admit, I want her. But there's still only one way to drive down this street, and that's the right way. You know how it is. The truth'll come back to bite you in the butt if you don't face it down to start with."

"Um, is that a Texas saying?"

She grinned. "No, but it should be, don't you think?"

"What I think, Ms. Raye, is that you've got too much on your plate—and that's a problem that you'd be really, really stupid not to let me help you with. What the hell good is it to have a friend with a ton of money unless you use him now and then? You know my house. You know Myrt, my housekeeper. And while you're trying to work full-time—"

"No," she interrupted firmly.

"No? No? This 'no' is in reference to what? I never asked you a question."

Since Sheila was nowhere in sight, Winona got up herself and carted their plates to the old Formica counter, out of their way. The baby was still snoozing, but starting to stir. With a little more space, she could use a hand to keep the baby carrier in a gentle, rocking motion, but her gaze stayed glued on Justin's. "Somehow you managed to get me talking all this time about Angel and my problems, Doc. But that isn't why I wanted to see you today."

She could see him brace, his eyes pick up a wary glint. "Yeah. I suspect you wanted to talk to me about weddings."

She nodded. "You're not going to bamboozle me into a marriage, Doc," she said gently.

"Do you think you're announcing something I didn't know? Why on earth would I want to bamboozle you into anything?"

But she was all through being fooled by that easy, lazy teasing tone. "That's exactly what confounded me for the last few days. Trying to understand. You've asked me to marry you a gazillion times, but I always knew you didn't mean it. I mean, it's one of our favorite private jokes together. But this time—you sounded serious. So then I started thinking. Maybe something was really bothering you." She watched his eyes. "I know something happened to you in Bosnia."

He stilled. "What is this? A guy can't ask a woman to marry him without her thinking he's mentally ill or has some deep dark problem?"

"Don't even try throwing feathers in front of my eyes, Doc. You know perfectly well that's not what I meant. Answer the question. Or is Bosnia something you can't talk about?"

She'd seen that exasperated look on his face before—and that unwilling hint of humor in his eyes. Somehow, some way, they'd always been able to talk honestly together. Even when Justin fought it tooth and nail. He threw up a hand. "How Bosnia got in this conversation beats me. But yeah, of course things happened to me there. I went through a year of real hell."

She nodded gently. "I know you did. And you've always pretty openly admitted that…but I meant, was there something that happened that you didn't talk about? Or couldn't? I know you saw horrors. I know you went through hell. But you came home and changed from trauma medicine to plastic surgery."

"So?"

"So…when I realized that, I tapped into my memory banks and it seemed like that was around the time that other things changed for you, too. You picked up a reputation as a devil-may-care playboy. It's stupid."

"I don't know about stupid. More, hard to avoid. I've got money and I'm single, so the press naturally—"

"Don't try to sell me cow patties, darlin'." Winona leaned forward, feeling better now. In fact, feeling downright good, now that the subject was off her and on him, and Justin was no longer looking at her as if she were whipped cream. "I'm talking about how the media regularly pegs you, Doc. I'm talking about the kind of reputation that you've let happen. And it isn't at all true."

"It's not exactly a *lie* that I'm single. Or that I have the means to—"

She snorted. Not particularly delicately. "You make out like you spend all your time on tummy tucks and boob implants. Nothing wrong with boob implants, mind you—but why is it that no one in town realizes you're the reason we have that fancy Burn Unit at Royal Memorial?"

"Who told you that?" Justin yanked on his ear, a clear clue that he was feeling edgy. "And for the record, I do my share of tummy tucks and nose jobs. If you think I'm apologizing for that—"

"No one's suggesting you need to apologize. If anything, you should take a bow. Some idiots think tummy tucks and boob jobs are about nothing but vanity. You've always been a women's supporter for real, Justin. Reconstruction after cancer or a tumor can make a difference to a woman's esteem…." Abruptly she stopped and waved that subject aside. She could have ranted on, but he was obviously trying to distract her. "Anyway, the point is—I'm not knocking the work you do. I'm only asking why you give the community the impression that you only take on spoiled rich women for patients, when in reality you donate a ton of your time to some of the worst burn cases over three states."

"Hell." He tugged on his ear again. "Who told you *that?* Someone's been spreading vicious lies and slander about me."

"Shut up, Justin. I'm just trying to tell you…I know something's wrong. Maybe it's not my business. But once I started realizing how much you've changed since Bosnia, it just kept hitting me in the face. Obviously something serious has been bothering you. Something you don't talk about. And I don't know whether that wild-assed idea about marrying me could be part of that, but…"

As if she hadn't been right in the middle of an important, serious conversation with him, Justin suddenly bolted to his feet and grabbed his jacket. Some instinct made Winona turn around in bewilderment, seeking some reason for his sudden behavior.

At the door to the diner, Willis Herkner was just ambling in. The jerk was still working for *American Investigator,* which, as far as Winona was concerned, was the belly-buster of all the sensational media rags. Willis was dressed to impress, wearing a long white aviator scarf with his ultracool jacket. Still, even though the smarmy investigator was a major nuisance, Winona couldn't fathom why his appearance would bother Justin enough for him to be hustling double-time out of there.

"Justin…" she began, intending to question him, but just then Angel's baby-blue eyes fluttered open and her rosebud mouth opened in a squeal. The first squeal was fairly sleepy and friendly sounding. The next one, Winona knew, wouldn't be. The baby needed to be fed, bathed and rocked to sleep. Come to think of it, after this long day—so did she.

Justin, in the meantime, had lunged out of the booth and was zipping up. "You know what? Even when you were a belligerent, aggravating, sullen twelve-year-old, I realized this odd thing about you. You were never fooled by people's bologna. You always saw past the cover story to the truth. I could never lie to you, Win, even when I wanted to."

"Well...that's good," she said forcefully, and then hesitated. He'd seemed to mean a compliment, didn't he? Only he'd managed to confuse her by the side comment. She organized the thoughts in her mind again, determined to get back to the point—there was something wrong, something bothering Justin, and she was determined to get him to talk about it.

Instead, faster than she could get the words out, he leaned down.

Half the town—maybe more—was sardine-packed in the Royal Diner, most of them familiar, the baby squawking louder now, children screaming from another booth and Sheila shrieking something to Manny in the back. Yet he kissed her. Just bent down, and softer than the stroke of a petal, brushed his lips on hers.

Like a rose hungry for sunlight, her whole body strained upward for the touch of him. Her throat arched at the same time her eyelashes swooshed down. It wasn't dark behind her closed eyelids. If anything, there were fireworks of light and soft, silver flames. Her closed eyes just cut out the riffraff sensory images in the restaurant until there was nothing in her mind—nothing in her sight, sound, touch, taste, but Dr. Justin Webb and his wicked, wicked mouth.

Her conscience scrambled for some common sense. Some inhibitions. Some sanity.

Nobody home behind any of those doors.

Oh my, oh my. She didn't let go. Not with men, not with anyone. You get too close to people, then if they abandoned you—even if they never meant to or wanted to—your heart broke. You didn't die. Your heart just hurt and ached and never stopped aching. Nothing was worth that. She was sure of that yesterday, and she was sure of it today.

But her lips clung to Justin's and wouldn't let go. Her hands didn't touch him. Her breasts, her legs, her tummy—no body part was connected to him except her lips. And tongue. His warm, silky tongue touched hers, gentle as a spring breeze, not demanding, not taking, just...offering. Touch. Taste. The intimacy of himself.

Heat flushed her body head to toe.

The baby revved up the volume of tears. A child galloped past toward the rest room. A plate clattered on the floor. The jukebox twanged out another song about pickup trucks and getting up in the morning. Neon lights flashed on, off, on, off into the dark winter night street outside. Winona saw. She heard. She just didn't care.

And then Justin lifted his head, eyes suddenly darker than a midnight sky. "It's a good idea, don't you think? Kissing in public."

"What?" He might as well have suggested rolling naked in a mud puddle. It would have made as much sense.

"Everyone in town realizes that we know each other, Win. But just in case...this way they'll get the picture that we're close...that we were thinking about getting married even before Angel entered the picture. This way we'll look like a couple. So it won't seem contrived or hokey when we tie the knot."

"Tie the knot," she echoed.

"And you're damn right. There was a very serious reason I asked you to marry me. It's because I thought we could make it together. And I thought that ages before you ever laid eyes on our beauty here."

He touched Angel's cheek, which was enough to startle her from whimpering into a gurgle for him. And then he strode for the door.

All that noise, all that chaos, but there suddenly wasn't a sound in the restaurant but the scratched tape from the jukebox. Some folks were being polite. But the others were either outright staring at her or at Justin's departing figure.

Swiftly, Winona gathered up the baby, patting, soothing, trying to grab her jacket and car keys at the same time. He put a drug in his kisses. Well, what else could she possibly think? Maybe she didn't recognize the controlled substance, but it was there. In the taste of him. The mood. The look in his eyes. And whatever was in that damn chemical went straight to her head.

And it was still going straight to her head.

Blasted man—richer than a tycoon—yet he'd forgotten to pay for their dinners. So she had to finagle that money out of her pocket, get her jacket on, get Angel and all the baby paraphernalia, all under the watchful, smiling eyes of everyone in the whole darn diner.

But when she finally hurtled into the night a few moments later, she sucked in a lungful of frigid winter air and, out of absolutely nowhere, smiled, too.

There was nothing funny about her situation. Nothing. She needed to figure that man out, and pronto. Somehow there still seemed to be a marriage proposal hanging between them. More worrisome yet was the stunning, startling thought that he actually *wanted* to marry her. But boy…

That man sure could kiss.

Six

Justin drove to the Texas Cattleman's Club, but when he parked the Porsche, he turned the key and sat there, motionless. His meeting with the guys was at eight. It was already a few minutes after. He could see lights on within the building, recognize some of the other members' cars in the lot. His mind needed to be on the plane crash and the missing jewels and serious business. Instead, all he could think about was Winona.

He was so in love with her.

Technically, loving her was old news. Heaven knew, he'd figured out his feelings for her long, long before he'd kissed her in the diner.

But that kiss was the first time he'd really dreamed, thought, *believed* that she could come to feel the same way about him. The baby was the first need he'd seen in Winona, the first dent in her emotional armor, the first emotion that she'd willingly revealed to him…but that kiss wasn't anything about Angel. It was about *them*. About something new and strong and powerful building between the two of them.

Justin tapped his fingers on the steering wheel, thinking that when a man got a taste of heaven, it was tough not to want it all. Both the problems and the joys. It was possible that Winona wanted to adopt every abandoned kid in the county for the rest of their lives, and God knew the woman was stubborn, closed in, too independent to lean on him even when he damn well wanted to be leaned on. But he really didn't care. Justin was also well aware that she was confused about the emotions suddenly exploding between them, but just as Shakespeare had said, all was fair in love and war. She'd been doing a lulu act on his heart for a long time. It wouldn't kill Win to be off balance for a bit.

Not when the cause was right.

Whistling, he finally climbed out of his classy chassis, and hiked toward the building. When he stepped inside, his mood promptly sobered.

He had to quit thinking about Win. For that matter he had to quit thinking like a cockeyed dimwit in love. This was no time to be singing in the rain.

He could hear a game of poker going on in the far room, saw a few men putting on their coats, leaving the card room where cigar smoke gushed out in a fog. From old habit, his eyes shot to the Leadership, Justice and Peace motto on the far wall. The actual sign wasn't that intrusive or large; most strangers ambling in rarely seemed even to notice it. But for him, it was like making eye contact with an old friend, and abruptly he charged toward the east rooms, expecting to find the others in the standard meeting area off to the right...and he did.

The room was as comfortably overloaded with testosterone as a room could get. A fire blazed in the hearth. A boar's head hung over the stone mantel. The pool table stood under a Tiffany chandelier, untouched, rack ready. The furniture was all leather, couches and big chairs, with ottomans to put your boots on—but no one was sitting tonight. Justin braced, feeling how much tension the others were giving off. Matt was pacing like a caged cougar, Dakota standing in the window, pensive and still. Aaron still wasn't back from Washington, but Ben was here now…typically, the sheikh had on his proper kaffiyeh for a serious meeting, and any other time Justin would have smiled. Ben was an extraordinary man who'd become a special friend, but he *did* have a way of looking like a desert warrior, between his kaffiyeh and those fierce dark eyes and rigid posture.

"For someone who's usually never late, I can't seem to catch up with a clock today to save my life. I'm sorry if I kept you waiting." Justin strode in, feeling guilty as a shamed hound. "And hell, you're all looking as dark as a thunderstorm. Are we talking more bad news? Dakota, I take it you looked for the red diamond—"

"No. I came here earlier, intending to do just what we said—check on the red diamond and report back to the rest of you," Dakota said. "Only when I got here, I discovered there was a problem. The wine-cellar door was unlocked."

Justin swore under his breath. Dakota continued, "So I could have called you all, but it made more sense to wait until I informed Hank Langley as he is the owner of the Club. He said he'd inform the other members, but we five, including Aaron, would take the lead and handle the situation. So now we need to discover what's wrong together. Decide what to do together. And earlier, there were just too many people here. It made the most sense to hold up any further investigations until after dark, now. Once the poker game breaks up in the other room, we'll be the only ones here. I only wish we'd managed to get hold of Aaron before now, because I have a feeling we're going to need his advice."

Matthew rolled his shoulders, obviously trying to shrug off the tension kinks. He also helped fill Justin in. "In principle, finding the wine-cellar door unlocked shouldn't be that much of a shock. We already know someone stole the two stones. Obviously they got in here somehow.''

''Yes.'' Ben stepped forward. ''Except that the night watchman should have caught an unlocked door and reported something about it.''

''There was nothing in Riley Monroe's log in the last two nights?'' Justin asked.

''Nothing written in any way,'' Dakota said with frustration.

''Well, that's odd.'' Justin knew, as they all did, that the older night caretaker was a hundred percent dependable. Riley may never have been the sharpest knife in the drawer, but he was both reliable and loyal. ''In the meantime…we haven't been able to track down Aaron?''

''No.'' Matthew's tone expressed more frustration. ''We know that he's still in Washington—which wouldn't have to be a problem if we could just reach him at either the embassy or his hotel room. But the embassy acts like he's not expected, and if he's getting messages from the hotel, he's not calling back.''

''But we left word for him to contact one of us, ASAP,'' Dakota affirmed.

''Well, we know he'll call as soon as he can. It's just that with so many people involved from Asterland and Obersbourg on that downed plane—and now we presume potentially involved with our theft—well, we all know Aaron's the one with the diplomatic expertise and background.'' Justin half turned. All of them could hear voices in the hall, men's laughter, louder as they moved toward the door. On a mean cold night like this—and a weekday night besides—it was unusual that the weekly poker game hadn't already broken up. But they should be alone within minutes, judging from the departing sounds of the group in the hall. Right then Justin was just as relieved to have a few more moments to study the others, anyway. ''You all seem to sense that something's wrong. I mean—obviously—besides the crises we already know about.''

Matthew nodded immediately. ''There is.''

Dakota concurred. ''Something badly wrong.''

Ben nodded, too. ''I think we should wait until we are alone in the building for sure, but this is hard. Like waiting for a tornado. I feel there should be a sword in my hand. A gun. As if something were menacing in every shadow.''

''Sheesh. You guys are giving me the willies. Come on now,'' Justin said reassuringly, thinking that the group would calm down if they reviewed what they knew. ''We had a theft. How or why that happened, none of us know. But whoever took the two jewels was on the flight to Asterland for sure. And since we recovered two of the jewels, we're not only ahead of the robber, but he—or she—is very likely out of the country by now. In fact, as far as I know, there's almost no one still in Royal who was originally scheduled on that flight—''

''Robert Klimt,'' Ben said.

''Who's in a coma.''

''Lady Helena—'' Matthew reminded him.

''Who's still in the hospital, between her broken leg and the burns.''

Matthew frowned. ''There was someone else. The teacher. Pamela something—''

''Yeah, Pamela Miles, the teacher who was dancing with Aaron the night of the gala.'' Justin threw up his hands. ''You guys saw her, didn't you? Even if you don't know her. I mean, she's a thief like Walt Disney was a secret terrorist. There's no way she could have been our jewel robber. And another local person on the flight was Jamie Morris, but she was going to Asterland to be a bride, so she's hardly a likely thief.''

''Yeah, yeah.'' Dakota suddenly cracked a slow smile. He knew what Justin had been doing. He always did. Dakota never hesitated to take charge of anything—actually, no one ever had to sell any of the Club members tickets. But he'd mentioned before how naturally Justin took the healer role, somehow diffusing the stress from a situation so all of them could work together better as a team. "I haven't heard a sound since the door closed the last time a few minutes ago. I'm positive those were the last guests in the place. Lay on, Macduff. Let's get this search party in motion and find out what's what."

Ben led the way. Actually, there was nothing mysterious about the passageway. Justin, like the others, always felt that secrets were dangerous. The best place to guard something important to you was out in the open, being honest about it— the way they'd always been honest about the three priceless jewels in the town legend. Everyone knew the legend of the jewels. No one believed it.

Although one person, Justin realized from the weight of the two stones in his pocket, obviously had.

Down a hall, past the cloakroom and rest rooms, was the giant kitchen. Beyond the kitchen was an anteroom, a spacious pantry. Inside the pantry was a door leading down several steps to the wine cellar. And at the far end of the wine cellar was a spring-loaded door. Neither the door nor the door lock was hidden from sight; they just appeared to be a natural part of the cellar wall unless someone looked closer. But the door was where the key should have worked—the key they each had.

Unfortunately, as Dakota had already warned them, the lock was already open. The door click-sprang open with the simple pressure of his hand. Inside was a stone passage. Narrow, cold to iciness, dry. Illuminated by bald lightbulbs strung from the ceiling at regular intervals. The passageway wasn't as cold as the wind-bitter night, but chilly enough to make Justin shiver uneasily.

Back in the War with Mexico—when the original Texas soldier carrying the jewels had died—an adobe church had stood on this site in Royal. The church was the original mission to the area, which was why Tex Langley had bought the land next to it and formed the Club—to protect the area's heritage. The law itself wasn't so dependable in those old days.

Not now either, Justin thought. Which was really the core reason the group had originally formed and persisted in staying together. Laws in themselves had no way to right all wrongs—or protect everyone. There always seemed to be abandoned babies like Angel. Things that went wrong in peoples' lives. Things the law couldn't fix. Things no one could fix if someone didn't step in and make a commitment to trying.

"Oh hell, oh hell, oh hell," Dakota muttered.

Justin surged forward. His vision was blocked by the other men's broad shoulders, but he sensed this was a problem specifically for him from something in Dakota's tone of voice. From one heartbeat to the next, he became a hundred percent doctor. The instant he caught sight of the crumpled body on the floor, he recognized Riley Monroe. He crouched down and felt for a pulse, but from his first look, he already knew.

There hadn't been a pulse in a long time. Probably a few days. Too damn long to do anything for the Club's old caretaker.

Over his head, the others had started moving. "Check the box for the other jewel," Ben said in a tone full of grit.

Matthew responded, "No, the red diamond's gone, too. Nothing here."

Then Dakota spoke, his tone as quiet as a winter night. "Justin?"

Justin understood that Dakota—that all of them—were counting on him to come up with some answers. No one had said the word *murder*. But they all knew that's what had taken place. "Well…there's a blow on Riley's head, but I don't think that's what caused his death. I think he was knocked out, then something else done to him. Not a gunshot or a knife wound. There's no blood. My guess is, an injection of some kind—which would imply planning on the part of the murderer. And it's so cool down here that I can't guess for sure when this happened, but I would think a couple of days ago—''

''A couple of nights ago. You mean, the night the Asterland plane tried to take off?'' Ben asked.

Justin used his own jacket to cover Riley's face, and then looked up. ''Yes. That's my guess.''

All of them exchanged glances, but it was Matthew who sucked in a breath and summed it all up. ''What a mess. We've got a dead body, a stolen red diamond, a plane crash. Tell the cops, and we risk an international incident—the worst thing that could happen when Asterland just achieved an uneasy peace with Obersbourg. And we'd risk that without knowing if our jewel thief/murderer was an American or one of the Asterland people.''

''We also have no actual reason to believe that the plane crash has any relationship to the jewel theft,'' Dakota said. ''The two events could be completely coincidental.''

Slowly Justin stood up. ''That's really true,'' he said thoughtfully. ''In fact, if it weren't for the plane crash, we might not have known about the theft of the jewels for quite a while. Which makes me believe that the two incidents really might have had nothing to do with each other. But right now, I'm afraid none of that matters. We have to deal with Riley. We don't have any choice about calling in the authorities.''

''I know.'' Matt cocked a foot forward. ''But the question is, which authorities? Riley's been murdered. Obviously we have to call the cops. But does that mean we have to tell them everything related to the Texas Cattleman's Club and the three jewels and our whole history of missions around the world? The thing is, it's one thing to tell the cops about Riley—and another to make the whole situation public. I wish we had someone to give us advice from the inside. There are bigger problems here than just Riley's murder."

"I agree," Ben said. "I doubt any of us would want to withhold information. That is not the issue. But if we get embassies involved here, we have a new nightmare. And unless we guard some information on our past Texas Cattleman's Club history, we jeopardize all our goals and all we've tried to do. I think we need a cop to know the whole story. But it has to be someone we can trust. Any too-fast decisions could make the situation even worse."

Immediately Winona's face sprang into Justin's mind. "Well…the first thing we have to do is take care of Riley. But on the subject of someone we could trust in the police department, I have a suggestion—"

Just then, though, his hospital beeper went off. Justin mentally swore. He couldn't be in three places at once, yet it was one of those nights when he *had* to be.

Winona had the telephone plugged to her ear when Wayne's beefy face showed up in her office doorway. Her boss cocked a leg forward while she finished the call. With one hand, he scratched his chin as he surveyed the wreckage.

Back when, Royal had had no juvenile department—which had meant there'd been no office for Winona when she'd been hired, until she converted a supply closet. At the best of times, there was turnaround room for a small man. Right now, apart from files stacked chin-high and a desk whose surface hadn't seen light since the millennium, the room was draped ceiling-to-floor with baby paraphernalia—and Angel herself took up no small space between blankets and rattles and bottles. She blew an excited bubble just for Wayne, though.

Wayne sighed, heavily, from the doorway. "First time I've been able to catch up with you all morning. You heard? About Riley Monroe being murdered?"

"I sure did."

"I don't like trouble in my town, and this whole week, there's been nothing but." Wayne scratched his jowly chin. Again. "How long you keeping that baby in the office, Raye?"

Wayne was one of those dogs where his bark was bad, but his bite was far worse. "The baby hasn't stopped me from pulling a full load," she said defensively.

"I didn't say it had. But it will. I got two of those at home. I know how full-time they are. Now, where you think you're going with this, Winona?"

"You know where I'm going with this. I'm searching for the mother."

"That's not what I'm asking and you know it. You're already so attached to that kid it shows in your face. She's not yours. And you're skating a line—you know you are—on not releasing the baby to Social Services."

"They haven't pressed."

Occasionally, Wayne could be annoyingly logical. "Because this is Royal. And because it's you and everyone knows and loves you." Wayne grunted. "That doesn't mean that this is by the book, though, and you know how I feel on that. If a cop doesn't behave by the straight and narrow, how can we enforce a law for anyone else?"

"I'm not breaking any law."

"I know that. I didn't say you were. Quit ducking the issue."

She nodded. "I'm sorry." She *was* sorry. As difficult as her boss could be sometimes, Wayne had always been on her side, and she could see he wasn't enjoying this discussion any more than she was. "Okay. As far as where I'm going with this—I'm expecting to find the parents. And I'm not even close to being done with the parent search. But if that turns up bad news, I'd like to adopt Angel. Or if not adopt, foster."

"All right. At least that's a straight answer." Wayne washed a hand over his tired face. "You need something filled out about what kind of character you got, what kind of foster parent you'd make, that kind of thing, you come to me, Raye,'' he said gruffly.

She couldn't kiss the boss. It would be completely inappropriate, and he'd hate it besides. "Thank you," she said sincerely.

"Yeah, well. That's not the only reason I stopped by. Did you happen to know Riley Monroe?"

"I knew he was the night watchman at the Texas Cattleman's Club. And he bartended for them at a lot of parties. He always seemed like a nice man. I can't imagine him involved with any trouble. But I didn't know him personally."

Wayne nodded. "Well, your impression's like everyone's. He's the last person anyone'd think would get murdered. The thing is, there's no keeping the death out of the papers. Folks'll want to show up to show respect and all, especially because Riley had no family. But I want all details kept out of the media until the investigation's over. I want a lid kept on this. Tight. And I know nothing in homicide's directly your problem, but I still want everyone in the station on the same page. If the press hound you, don't say anything."

"No problem." Someone screeched that there was a phone call for Wayne, and he hiked back to his office, four-letter words spilling from his mouth like drool. It was one of those mornings when no one could catch their breath. She was just reaching for the phone herself when it rang, and she grabbed it.

"Winona?"

"Yes?" She was positive that she recognized the feminine voice—only not exactly.

"I'm at your house, dear—"

"I beg your pardon?"

"And I just wanted to know if there was anything that you're allergic to."

"Well, no, but—"

"Fine. I just didn't want to risk cooking something that

didn't suit you. And Justin didn't feel that you'd want me baby-sitting until the two of us had a chance to sit down and talk, but it's not like we're total strangers. So I did want to say right up front, I'm available. And I adore children. And I'll be here, helping in your house, anyway, so there's no problem if the baby were here, too. And that's all, dear. I realize that you're at work and probably aren't supposed to be getting personal calls. No problem.''

The woman abruptly hung up. Winona stared at the buzzing phone for several moments, feeling completely befuddled. Yes, the woman's voice was familiar, but she couldn't place it. And the whole conversation, covering cooking and allergies and baby-sitting—made no sense to Winona whatsoever. She might have been alarmed, particularly at the idea of a stranger being in her house—if someone's telltale name hadn't come up.

Justin.

A series of bubbles were cooing from the baby carrier on her desktop. "Angel," Winona said, "I think we'd better go home for lunch today. Is that okay by you?"

Angel kicked her feet, clearly thrilled at the thought.

At ten minutes after twelve, Winona took one last bite from a fast-food hamburger as she pulled into her driveway. An unfamiliar car was already parked there—an Olds. Gray. And the model was older, but the car was still kept up to within an inch of its life, with paint gleaming and white-walled tires cleaner than brand-new.

Feeling even more bewildered, Winona grabbed Angel from her car seat and whisked the diaper bag to her shoulder. The baby wasn't fussing, but she was going to any second. Angel was such an ultrasmart baby that she could already tell time. At 12:12 p.m. she was going to want a bottle. Not 12:14 p.m. Not 12:13 p.m. But at precisely 12:12 p.m., and as long as she got exactly what she wanted, Angel was possibly the most miraculous, perfect, congenial baby ever to have been born. And Winona would have loved her no matter what, but right then it seemed a good idea to run for the door.

As swiftly as she juggled the baby and her purse and the diaper bag and the back-door key, however, she abruptly discovered that the door was already unlatched. Her door. Unlocked.

One peek inside almost gave her a new reason for a heart attack.

There were no dirty dishes piled in the sink. The kitchen tile was scrubbed within an inch of its life. A sponge cake was cooling on the counter, and something savory was brewing on the stove. Winona didn't bake. And she sure as hell didn't make—or know how to make—French stews.

She tiptoed in a few more steps. Both the washing machine and dryer were churning in the utility room. More shocking yet, there were folded clothes on top of the dryer. Folded. Not heaped or hurled willy-nilly.

This was all pretty terrifying. Still, she unwrapped Angel from her jacket, then pushed off her own, and carried the baby through the rest of the house. Clearly there was an intruder. Clearly no good mother would risk her child when there was obviously a stranger in the house, but there was building evidence to Winona that this particular intruder was mentally ill. Not in a dangerous way. Just in a distinctive way.

There wasn't a single towel on the floor in the bathroom. Not one. There were no stockings, no slips, no jeans piled on the floor in her bedroom. The bed was made. *Made.* With clean sheets. Like real people lived.

Holding the baby protectively close, she tiptoed toward the living room—where she already knew the intruder was, from the violent roaring sound. Sure enough, there was a woman's rump, bent over her couch, pushing the vacuum cleaner beneath it.

As if finally sensing there was someone else in the house,

the woman suddenly jumped, whirled, slapped a hand on her chest and turned off the roaring vacuum at the same time.

"Don't be frightened," Winona said warmly. "I can help you with this. I know there has to be a recovery program for cleaners. There is for every other problem. If nothing else, I can be your support group. Trust me, I can teach you to live with dirt. I know. I do it every day—"

The woman dropped the hand from her chest and let out a guffaw…followed by a second guffaw and then a full belly laugh. "Justin always said you were full of the devil. You do remember me, don't you? Myrt?"

"Of course I do." Even if all the clues hadn't come together, Winona would have recognized Justin's housekeeper when she finally got a good look.

It wasn't as if they really knew each other, but Myrt wasn't the kind of person anyone forgot. The jeans and T-shirt fit the figure of a thirty-year-old, but the worn, leathered face looked more like sixty, creased with both life and laugh lines. Huge silver earrings dangled from her ears when she leaned forward to catch a glimpse of Angel.

"So that's our baby, huh? Just for the record—I had four of my own. And seven grandkids now. But I hardly get to see the children. Everybody moved so far away with their jobs and all. I get so hungry to hold a baby."

Winona was slowly picking up the picture of what was going on here—but she wasn't completely sure. "Our baby," she echoed.

"Uh-huh." Warm brown eyes met hers. Winona was smart, but she had a bad feeling that Myrt was smarter. "Justin said you had your hands way too full, trying to work full-time and take care of the baby, too. Said you were getting worn out. His house is big, but it's nothing to clean, pretty much because he's never there. Truthfully, he has so much room that it would be much easier to set up you and the baby at his place—"

"Whoa." Winona could feel her knees giving way.

"—but it doesn't matter to me. He's paying me a ton—which, of course, is only half of what I deserve—because I'm the best grandma you'll ever hire. I bake like a dream. Never lose patience with a child. And I love to clean—"

"You're frightening me," Winona said baldly.

"Now, now. Pretty darn silly for you to look a gift horse in the mouth, isn't it? You need the help. I'm here. And Justin's paying my salary, so it's not like you have to worry about it. I can sleep over any time you want—"

"Whoa. Double whoa."

"Truthfully, I wish my nights weren't so free, but since Ted died...well, there's still heat in this old furnace, but I just can't seem to look at another man. I've tried. The point being, though, that I can stay all night with our Angel if you need me to. It's no problem at all. Truthfully, it's better for the baby to be in her own environment than taken out to a baby-sitter's. Now, let's get down to the important stuff. How often does she want a bottle? When's her bath time? Her fussy time?" Myrt waggled her fingers, signaling that she wanted Winona to fork over the baby.

Winona carefully handed her Angel, then stood as rigid as a school principal, watching every movement the other woman made. She didn't hold Angel the way Winona did. Didn't pat her exactly the same way, either. Nothing was remotely perfect. But the woman was clearly enamored big-time the instant she touched the baby, and Angel was cooing right back.

"Myrt?"

"Hmm?" The woman had dropped the vacuum cleaner and sat down with the little one. Clearly work and cleaning were forgotten. Winona's respect for her upped ninety notches.

"She gets cranky around dinner. Actually, it's no set time. Just whenever I'm trying to eat. And other than that, she almost never cries unless she's got a good reason. On food, though, she wants a bottle every four and a half hours, and I do mean pronto—and she's a minute overdue right now.''

''Well, then, I'll get it. We're going to have a great time together, aren't we, precious?'' Myrt seemed to have lost all interest in paying attention to Winona.

''Well, I don't want to leave you, but as soon as she gets this bottle, she's likely to drop off for almost a two-hour nap. And I really need to have a talk with Justin. Would you mind if I took off for just a bit?''

''Well, of course not, dear. That's what I've been telling you. I'm here for you. And the baby.''

Winona grabbed her jacket and car keys and hightailed it outside. As soon as she climbed in her car, she cell-phoned her boss so Wayne would know she wouldn't be at her desk for a while.

Possibly ''a while'' was an understatement, she mused, as she shot out of the driveway. When she caught up with Justin…well, when she caught up with Justin, she wasn't quite sure *what* she was going to do to him.

But she was going to do it *good*.

Seven

When Winona pushed open the door to Royal Memorial Hospital, her pulse was hurtling at a hundred miles an hour. Heaven knew why she was so nervous when the chances were slim that she'd even find Justin. He could easily be tied up for hours in surgery, and it wasn't as if she would ever interrupt him when he was busy with patients.

She didn't *have* to see him this instant, Winona kept telling herself. For darn sure he shouldn't have sicced Myrt on her without asking permission, but being good to her was hardly a murdering offense. She could yell at him about that any old time, and, yes, it troubled her that they still hadn't settled the proposal question, but that was part and parcel of the same problem. Something was wrong with Justin. He was behaving in very odd, very troubling ways. She wanted—needed—to get to the root of all this nonsense, but grabbing him at work for a snatched conversation was never going to resolve any of that.

She should be home. Or at her own work. Anywhere but

clipping down the hall toward the Plastic Surgery/Burn Unit hell-bent for leather—and still she kept bounding along at the same breakneck pace. Although a number of familiar faces called out a "Hey, Winona!" she avoided making eye contact or anything but a brusque return greeting. Everyone in town knew she was a cop, and she roamed the hospital floors at all hours without anyone ever saying boo, so she had no fear that anyone would stop or question her. Nerves were hammering on her conscience, though. She knew perfectly well that she had no excuse in God's great earth to be here. She just wanted to see him.

And for some unknown reason, she wanted to see him *now*. Not later. To yell at him for being manipulative and bossy, she told herself virtuously.

But even having given herself a good, sound, self-righteous excuse didn't seem to stop her heart from hammering.

She paused at the nurses' desk right inside the Plastic Surgery unit. "You haven't seen Dr. Webb, have you?" she asked a nurse in ice-blue scrubs with Mary Jo on her chest badge.

The blonde recognized Winona with a tired smile. "He's been in here off and on since last night. You know, the accident with the two teenagers on Cold Creek Road? Stevie really got his face cut up."

"Aw, hell," Winona said. "Stevie Richards?" As if there were more than one Stevie living on Cold Creek Road.

"Yeah. Parents called Dr. Webb right away last night. The whole family was just a mess. Dr. Webb finally kicked them all out, sat with Stevie himself after the surgery, got him calm, kept him calm...." Normally Mary Jo would never have told a patient's business, but Winona had known her for years. She generally knew more about an accident or a kid's problems than ever made it on a hospital's records, so the two frequently exchanged notes and information. "Anyway, I knew he wasn't in Stevie's room an hour ago, but I can—''

Winona could see her hand reaching for the phone. ''No, don't call him. I don't want to bother him if he's with a patient. This wasn't that important.'' If Justin had been up all night, he had to be exhausted. That changed things. Her need to see him was some kind of emotional thing, but that was foolishness. Win was an ace pro at putting emotions in the bank when she didn't absolutely have to spend them.

''Well, he's still in the hospital, I know.'' Mary Jo tapped a finger on the desk. ''I'm pretty sure he was headed up to Lady Helena's room. At least, he mentioned wanting to do a consult with Dr. Harding and Dr. Chambers. That was about a half hour ago, so I'm guessing you might have picked a good time to catch him.''

''Thanks. I owe you.''

Outside, she heard the whir of a helicopter. Royal Memorial was hardly a metropolis-size hospital, but the Burn Unit had begun earning a stellar reputation from the day it opened, and these days patients were often flown in from other cities. Still, the minute she walked into the Burn Unit, it was like wandering onto another planet. All the noise and hustle of the Emergency Room disappeared. Here, it was quiet. A gentle place, with pale blue walls and soft lighting. Nobody sneezed here, no one coughed—Winona had always figured that no one would dare. Justin would shoot anybody who came in here with a cold, because even bitsy germs could be a serious threat to a burn patient. The smells were the same old hospital smells—alcohol and bleach and antiseptics—but somehow neither the quiet nor the stinks made for a cold atmosphere. If you were a patient here, you were in big trouble. You needed peace and serious healing. And that's how Winona always felt here, as if she were in a place designed to soothe the spirit as well as heal the body.

Somehow, for a while now, she'd intuited that Justin needed that kind of healing place as well—that he hadn't created the Burn Unit just from studies of how a good one should be, but from something inside himself. Some sore that he hid from sight.

That thought was still on her mind when she located him.

Lady Helena's room was supposed to be a secret for security reasons—she was one of the most seriously VIP patients the hospital had ever had—but every cop in town knew where she was. When Winona rounded the corner, she recognized Dr. Harding and Dr. Chambers. They were both standing in the doorway, and she could hear Justin's voice from inside the room.

Dr. Chambers was the bone man. He wasn't the chattiest guy in town, but Winona had taken him busted-up kids before, knew he was an okay guy.

Dr. Harding was a woman and impossible not to like. Her specialty was burns, and the compassion in her eyes created its own kind of beauty. Justin never took credit for a damn thing, but Winona'd heard through the grapevine that he'd stolen Dr. Harding from Boston because of her innovative work with burn patients.

Winona hesitated at the far end of the hall, wary of coming closer and intruding. Because the town rehashed every ounce of news related to the plane crash every morning at the Royal Diner, she basically knew what had happened to Lady Helena. Helena had suffered burns as well as a severely broken ankle in the crash. Justin had been a consult on her medical team from the get-go, even though she wasn't in his direct hands yet. The break had to be healed and so did the burns, before he could do plastic surgery for the scars. Winona remembered exactly how beautiful Lady Helena was, how graceful and elegant she'd come across to everyone at the Texas Cattleman's Club gala. Now, her voice inside the hospital room was pale and groggy and frightened.

"When can I go home?"

"I'm afraid you're stuck with us for a while. Weeks yet.

But I promise, we'll do our best to keep you entertained,'' Dr. Harding teased gently.

''I'll have use of my hand? My leg again?''

The two doctors in the hallway exchanged glances. ''We believe so, Helena.'' And then they walked out, down the hall in the other direction, leaving Justin alone with Lady Helena.

''Doctor Webb, what am I going to look like? Please tell me the truth. No one else seems willing to answer a direct question. I can't deal with the truth if I don't know what it is. How bad are the scars going to be?''

Right then, Winona almost spun around and took off. She completely changed her mind about talking to Justin. It would wait. It was just selfishness, her wanting to see him, to be with him. And it was now obvious that he'd had a harrowing night and was having an even tougher day—Lady Helena's careful, softly voiced questions could darn well break any woman's heart—and Winona just couldn't imagine bugging him right now.

Still, she lingered, just for a few more moments. Not to bug him. Not even to wait for him. But even though she couldn't make out his specific words to Helena, she could hear him talking, the cadence of his voice like the refrain of an old love song, gentle, familiar, soothing. And then he was striding out, his head bent as he stuck a pen in his white hospital coat, the smile for his patient still plastered on his face…but that smile disappeared the instant he moved out of Helena's sight.

He clearly believed that he was alone in the hall for that second. Winona could see those proud shoulders of his sag, the starch go out of his posture. His good-looking face was darn near chalk-white from exhaustion.

There was no way she was walking away from him.

''Justin?''

Even before his head whipped around at the sound of her voice, he had his normal expression back in place. His spine automatically straightened; his mouth tipped in that Sam El-liot, lazy, almost-smile; the virile vitality clipped back in his step. And those gorgeous eyes looking her over were—nat-urally—opaque as far as revealing any of his own feelings.

"Sheesh, Win. You prowling the bad neighborhoods again, looking for trouble?"

That was the whole problem with his teasing. She either wanted to smack him—or kiss him. The bottom line, as she was coming to realize, was that no matter what, she had always been tempted to touch him. How could she have failed to notice that for so long? "You had to know I'd track you down, after what you did," she said severely.

"What, what? I didn't do anything."

"Don't try that innocent routine on me, Doc. You're in trouble—and most people know better than to get in trouble with a cop. It's time to face the music. Exactly what do you still have to do this afternoon?"

"Well, I'm done with patients for the day, but I think I was supposed to meet with some insurance woman this af-ternoon. And I've got a good two hours of paperwork." He shot her a wayward grin. "I can cancel that stuff. I'd rather get in trouble with you any old time. But I have to admit, Win, I can't promise to be any kind of great company. I'm a little on the tired side."

A little? That wayward grin couldn't fool her in a month of Sundays. The more she studied him, the more she realized that he'd be lucky to drive himself home without falling asleep at the wheel. "Well, I promise, I only want a few minutes of your time—"

He frowned abruptly, as if suddenly remembering some terribly serious thing. "Actually, I need to talk to you. Se-rious talk. In fact, I wanted to call you much earlier, but stuff kept happening at the hospital and I just couldn't get free to make the call. I'm glad we ran into each other—"

Winona was afraid it was weddings he wanted to talk about. That wasn't going to happen. Now that she realized how completely wasted he was, his fate was sealed as far as how this encounter was going to go. "Okay, I'll tell you what. Let's swing by your house. Grab a sandwich. We can talk while you're eating and then I'll hightail it home."

His eyebrows raised. "That plan works great for me, but it doesn't seem very convenient for you. Since when do you want to go to my place?"

Since never. She'd been there; she knew where he lived, but she'd never felt comfortable alone with him in his house. It wasn't a matter of not trusting Justin—in any way—but of always feeling edgy with the feelings he stirred in her. But right now none of that mattered. The only issue was getting Justin fed, comfortable, and asleep, which she figured would be a lot easier to manipulate on his own turf.

She followed his Porsche, which gave her a chance to use her cell phone to call Myrt. "How late can you stay?"

"I told you, I told you. All night, if you need me to. Any time."

"Well…how's Angel?"

"Just like her namesake."

"Being good?"

"Happy as a clam."

Winona's worry nerves detangled. "Well, the thing is, I just caught up with Justin and he's really whipped. What I'd like to do is take him home and make sure he gets some rest, but I know he won't go along if I tell him that plan. I can't believe I'm going to be at his place for very long, but I just can't give you an exact time when I'll be home."

"So this is easy. I know where you are, I'll call you if I need you. Otherwise, take the evening off, mom. Go play. If you're not back by the time I get tired, I'll just bunk down in the spare bedroom and leave the door cracked so I can hear the baby. Now, do you have a key?"

Winona blinked at the phone. Even her foster mothers had never asked if she'd had a key. Myrt was like having an honorary mother—whether she wanted one or not.

But her humor suffered a fadeout when she pulled up behind Justin in his drive. Her house was only a couple miles from here, but it might as well be another universe. His place was white stucco with a Spanish red-tile roof, two stories tall with pillars framing the front door. A covered patio stepped down in layers to water gardens. Her yard had a clothesline. His had a marble fountain and a jetted pool.

When he unlocked the door, he ushered her in first. Possibly it was the sudden silence that made her so oddly nervous. She scuffed off her jacket, pushed off her shoes, tried to brazen past her nerves with some normal conversation. "It's been a while since I've been here. In fact, I don't think I've ever been upstairs—how many rooms up there?"

"Four bedrooms and three baths, I think—but I can't swear to that," he said wryly. "I haven't been up there myself since I can remember."

She shot him a bemused smile. "And that's another question I never got around to asking you before—why on earth did you buy such a big house?" The downstairs alone was a maze of room choices. Past the dining and living areas were a den and office, a sunroom and game room, and somewhere on the first floor was the master bedroom as well.

"Beats me. At the time, it seemed to make sense. I wanted a house in town, close to the hospital and my office. But I didn't want a place in the same neighborhood as my parents—I love 'em, but that'd be too close. And as much as I'm crazy about my grandparents' ranch, I couldn't see living in the country. It's just too far from my work."

"But you didn't need anything this monster size!"

"Well, I know. But Myrt and the gardener both came with this place. And the closed staircase made it easy to shut off the upstairs, so I have all that extra space for company, but it doesn't get dirty or messed up if I just stay out of it. I really do like the room, though. And that brothers and sisters and family can pile in here over the holidays."

She took a breath, but Hell's bells...there was no way to

get a question answered if you didn't ask it. "Were you thinking about a house big enough for a family when you bought it?"

His head shot up. For a moment, she forgot how tired he was. The look of awareness kindling in his eyes seemed as electric and wide-awake as a charge of lightning. "If you're asking if I can imagine you and our kids living here—yes, I can. And yes, I have been. Although imagining you and I practicing how to make those kids is mostly what's been on my mind."

She was a cop. Too old and too life-smart to blush, but blast the man if she didn't feel warmth surging up her cheeks. No matter how close they'd become—no matter that there was a marriage proposal between them. She still couldn't seem to believe that he wanted her. Or that she hadn't realized how much fire had been simmering between them for so many years without her knowing. "Justin, I wasn't asking about us—"

He grinned, but he also quit teasing. "Yeah, I know, you were asking me why I bought the house. But the truth is...I don't know, Win. At the time, I just liked the place. It wasn't that practical a decision. I fell for the two fireplaces and the unbeatable pool table in the game room. And the two trees in here."

There were. The two fringey trees in his great room stretched at least ten feet tall. He flipped on switches as they walked through. Recessed lighting immediately softened the darkness, illuminating the picture windows and vaulted ceiling, the hardwood floor, the giant furniture—couches, chairs, cushions—all upholstered in a thick, white cotton duck. Most of the color in the room came from true-life greens—not just the trees, but also bushy plants in tubs.

Her gaze swept from the plants and white furniture to the occasional splashes of contemporary art on the walls. "Did you choose all this yourself?"

"Are you kidding? Mostly the house came this way. All

I had to do was water the plants and pick out some stuff for the walls.''

"Men," she murmured dryly.

"Hey." Still headed for the kitchen, he pushed on more switches. A gas fire suddenly sizzled in the great-room hearth, adding warmth and light. They passed a hall table heaped with mail. A door opening onto his office. The downstairs bathroom looked more like a sitting room for a sultan than a practical john. She only caught a fast glimpse of the lapis lazuli tile, the square tub with whirlpool, the blanket-size towels in cobalt.

"I've got that color blue, too, but somehow it doesn't look quite the same at my budget level."

"I keep telling you to marry me, don't I? Then you could get your hands on all my money. Doesn't that sound good?"

Getting her hands on him sounded good. Too good. Particularly for a woman who had never considered herself sex-obsessed before—but just then she had other priorities. Justin was barely walking straight. He was weaving-tired, groggy-voiced tired, his teasing even sounding slurred.

When they passed by the game room—right before the kitchen—she flipped on the light switch herself, because she strongly suspected they'd end up in there. It was so obviously Justin's nest. Between floor-to-ceiling windows were floor-to-ceiling bookcases, all crammed to the gills with dog-eared volumes. The pool table sat in the room's center, and the hearth in here wasn't gas, but had real wood stashed in bins by the side. The old Oriental rug under the table was as thick as a sponge, and the far couch was red leather, a dark cranberry, as warm as the lantern lamps on the mantel top.

The look of that room lingered in her mind as she walked into the kitchen. Without giving Justin a chance to start talking, she promptly pushed her sleeves up and put her hands on her hips. "Okay, you, it's your lucky day. While you get a chance to shower and put your feet up, I'm volunteering to cook. I'll make anything you want—as long as it's no tougher than melted cheese sandwiches and potato chips. No, no, don't thank me. I realize you're used to Myrt making you riff-raff gourmet stuff, but out of the goodness of my heart, I'll even add Oreos for dessert—''

''Um, could I change my mind about loaning you Myrt and get her back?''

''No.'' She used the royal pointing figure to motion him toward his bedroom and bath. She didn't want Myrt touching the conversation. Or even teasing hints about marriage. Not until the damn man had some food and rest. For Pete's sake, he had bags under his eyes bigger than boats. ''Go. Get cleaned up.''

''Did I know you were this domineering and abusive before?'' he asked plaintively—but he obeyed and left, even if she did hear him chuckling all the way down the hall.

She prowled his kitchen for the ingredients for their make-shift dinner. By the time he emerged from the shower, rubbing a towel in his hair, barefoot, wearing clean jeans and a loose, long-sleeved T-shirt, she had a tray of food set up in the game room. A small fire hissed and snapped in the stone hearth. She'd lit the lanterns on the mantel, and the glow shone on the cheese-and-bacon sandwiches and chips.

''Hell. This is almost as good as fast food. Myrt's always making me eat nutritional kind of stuff.''

''I had a feeling that you really suffered regularly with her cooking.''

''She bosses me around worse than...'' he yawned as he plopped down on the leather couch, ''...my mom.'' He glanced at her with an owlish expression. ''Man, I'm sorry, Win. I should probably make some coffee. I know I'm lousy company.''

''Forget the coffee,'' she said gently, thinking that if he made a move toward caffeine, she just might have to sit on him. ''Just eat a little, okay? Then lean back. Watch the fire for a while. It won't kill you to take ten, will it?''

"No, but I have to talk to you. About something important. Really important."

She figured this talk was about marriage—and really, she agreed. It was time they settled that wild proposal of his. He deserved an answer. And tonight was one of the first times in a blue moon she'd had him alone to talk privately—but not right then. Darn it, he was beyond exhausted.

He wolfed down two sandwiches and a glass of iced herbal tea, leaned back with a sigh, and just like that, he was out. His eyes closed, and he dropped off faster than a worn-out baby.

With a quiet triumphant chuckle, she scooped up their few dishes, took care of those, then tiptoed back to the game room. She spotted a throw on a chairback, and gently tucked it around him, then curled up in the red leather chair at his side.

She had no intention of staying more than a few more minutes. Even if Myrt was all settled to take care of Angel, she wanted to get home, get back to the baby. But first she wanted to make sure that Justin was sound asleep, and that there was someone to field the phone or any other noises that could interrupt him for a while.

In a half hour, max, she was leaving.

For sure.

She woke up feeling disoriented. For a few moments she couldn't fathom where she was or how she'd come to be here, but gradually the details came into focus. She saw the yellow fire still sizzling in the hearth, recognized the rich Oriental carpet and the fancy pool table, finally realized that, of course, she was at Justin's...but then she felt it.

His gaze. On her face. Justin was sitting up, wide-awake but as silent and still as a secret, his dark, soft eyes on her face as if glued there.

She suffered through it again. That feeling. That feeling she never got with anyone else...of wanting to let go, of wanting to be abandoned. Not the dread-sick sensation of being deserted and alone, but the other meaning of abandoned, the kind that was a choice—a fierce desire to abandon everything familiar and safe and just feel. Him. From her toes to her chin. From deep in her belly. To explore and discover everything she might be with him if the lights were off—under the sheets.

Her throat was suddenly arid, her pulse suddenly pounding. Swiftly she tried to say something normal. "Hey, Doc. I take it we both fell asleep?"

"Uh-huh. You set me up, didn't you?" he accused her. "That's why you volunteered to come here. Because you knew I'd fall asleep the first chance I had to sit down."

"Yeah, I did set you up. But I'd heard you were up all night with that boy in the car accident. It wasn't going to kill you to be taken care of for a change."

"Yeah, well, two can play that manipulative game. I called Myrt earlier so she'd know where you were, said you'd fallen asleep. She said she already knew where you were, and the baby's fine and to stay put."

"What time is it?"

"A few minutes after two. Are you awake enough to talk about something serious?"

"Um…give me a five-minute time-out, okay?" She hightailed it out of the room, washed her hands, brushed her hair, slapped on lipstick, and came back with two mugs of instant coffee. "Now I'm ready," she said, but as she sat back down, she felt stiff with worry. What she wanted to do as far as Justin's marriage proposal, and what she thought they should do were two different things. While she was trying to marshal her thoughts into something tactful and coherent, though, he started talking.

"Win…I need to tell you about some jewels."

"Jewels?" She asked blankly.

"Yes. You know the old town legend? How back in the War with Mexico, one of our Texas boys, Ernest Langley, came across a wounded soldier and tried to save him. The man died, but our Ernest found three jewels on the old guy, brought them home to Royal, planned to live high on them— but the way life worked out, he didn't have to, because oil was discovered on his land. So he quietly donated the jewels to the old mission to secure the future of the town. Basically that was how the Texas Cattleman's Club came to be. The original founder, Tex Langley, grandson of Ernest, brought a group of men together who were charged with protecting the jewels, using them to keep the town prosperous and for the town's greater good through the generations. They built the Club right next to the old mission."

"Um, Justin? I was raised on that legend. Everyone in Royal knows it. Except for the part about the Texas Cattleman's Club, anyway." She was wide-awake now, but of all the things she was tensed up to discuss with him, old legends weren't remotely on the list.

"Just bear with me, okay? Those three jewels were an emerald, an opal and a diamond. Only, each of them were extraordinary jewels of their kind. The opal was a black harlequin, of a size and color that made it especially rare. It was an old tradition for judges to wear amulets of opal, because the stone was said to give the wearer the power of justice and healing."

"Um, Justin—"

"The emerald was a particularly big sucker, and through history, emeralds were considered the stone of peacemakers. Those first two gems were priceless to a collector, because they were so unusual in themselves, but the third stone was a red diamond. You see one, you'll likely never see another, because they're that rare, that precious. And red diamonds, of course, were symbolically the stones of kings, likely because only the most powerful men could possibly own them. So that's how we chose the sign for our Texas Cattleman's Club—Justice, Leadership and Peace. Because of those stones."

"Uh-huh. Justin—" she started impatiently.

"They were stolen."

"Ju— *What?*"

"The stones—the ones in the legend—were always real. So was the legend. It all happened. It was never just a story, it was always the truth. The soldier dying, our Texas boy finding the jewels, his grandson deciding to use them to secure the future of the town by forming the Texas Cattleman's Club. And over the years, the group has slowly, quietly taken on other kinds of protectorate roles. I'd like to think that there's always someone willing to stand up to protect the innocent. To step in when no one else wants to—or when there is no one else—to help someone who needs it."

Winona weakly waved a hand. "How about if you let me catch my breath for a second and a half? You just gave me a lot to take in. This is all related to where you disappear to sometimes, isn't it? The times you've let everyone think you're some kind of playboy doc, taking a spur-of-the-moment luxury cruise with your latest woman—"

"Nah. I don't do cruises. Every once in a while, maybe I do something for the group. But back to the theft of the jewels—"

"Yes. For God's sake. Let's go back to the theft—"

He hunched forward, looking serious again. "Someone on the flight to Asterland stole the jewels. We didn't know they were gone until four of our Club members went to examine the plane a few days ago. There was a reason we were included in the investigation. The Texas Cattleman's Club was involved in helping Princess Anna, had a leading role in getting those two countries talking again, so we were more familiar with their diplomatic problems and the personalities than any other outsiders—"

"Yes, that's why you had the whole party a few weeks ago."

Justin nodded. "And so far, no one has uncovered an explanation for the plane's mechanical problems—whether the problems were accidental or sabotage. Because there's been so much friction between the countries, obviously sabotage was, and is, a serious concern. The point, though, is that when we started searching for evidence on the plane, instead of finding clues to the mechanical problems—by complete accident, we found two of our jewels. The opal and the emerald.''

"My God." Her head was starting to reel from the implications of everything he was telling her.

Justin nodded again. "But we didn't find the red diamond. It's still missing. When the men went back to the Club—to the safe where the jewels were kept—we found the safe wide-open and Riley Monroe dead. Murdered. Apparently by the jewel thief.''

"Holy kamoly. I don't understand—''

"Neither do we, Win. That's why I'm telling you all this. The situation has gotten more touchy by the day. The group mutually determined that we need someone on the police force that we could absolutely trust...and naturally, you're it. As soon as I said your name, the others clicked with it.'' He scalped a hand through his hair. "I realize you're not directly part of the investigation related to Monroe's murder, but that's not the point.''

Winona stopped trying to talk. She was just listening. Hard.

"The complications just keep coming. For one thing, the last thing we want to do is publicly accuse anyone from Asterland or Obersbourg of stealing the jewels. Now that those two countries have finally achieved an uneasy peace, we don't want to fire up tempers again, or risk an international incident. But that means that the investigation into the jewel theft—and Riley Monroe's murder—needs to be done quietly. And tougher than that...'' Justin stood up with an impatient sigh and rolled his shoulders.

"...tougher than that...is that the Texas Cattleman's Club has kept the jewels a secret for generations now. For a good cause. We were able to keep our little expeditions and missions quiet, for the same reason. If we blow our cover, we blow our ability to help people—at least in the private ways we've been able to do in the past. If the truth about the jewels has to come out, then that's the way it is. But we'd rather it didn't get out. It would be different if we were just positive there was a connection between the plane crash and Riley's murder and the jewel theft. We're not. We don't know that. We don't know *anything* for sure. Not right now.''

Finally she could see where he was leading. ''Okay. You're obviously telling me this for a reason. What do you need me to do?''

In the intimacy of firelight, his gaze seemed to glow and soften on her face. ''Win...I don't like putting you on the spot. But until we sort this out, we need someone we can trust inside the police force. Someone who can help us evaluate what facts go where, help us keep things quiet that don't have to be public. Someone, for that matter, who can brainstorm with us over the clues we've got going...I don't mean that the police chief would be unaware of what we're asking you. But he's not our man, because there'd be nothing but a conflict of interest problem for him. We need someone else. Someone who's judgment we trust. Whose integrity we trust. We need the kind of person who everyone felt we could be comfortably and completely honest with—''

''Justin—?''

''What?''

She surged to her feet.

Eight

Winona wanted to wildly shake her head, as if to make absolutely positive that she'd heard him correctly. "You trust *me?*"

Justin had been pacing back and forth in front of the hearth, but now he stopped still, his brow furrowing. "Of course I trust you. What kind of question is that?" He hesitated. "The only worry I have is about putting you on the spot, Win. It's not fair. There's no reason you should feel obligated to help the Texas Cattleman's Club. This is their problem. My problem. I'm the one who brought your name up, and I should have been thinking about how this could affect you. At the time, the only issue on my mind was coming up with someone whose integrity and judgment I didn't question—and that's how all the guys felt, too. You just seemed the perfect one for us to ask. Everyone said the same thing. We all trust you, we all knew we could be comfortable and honest with…"

He abruptly stopped talking as if distracted by her sudden,

swift charging across the room toward him. Maybe she was just stumbling across the Oriental carpet, but she felt as if she were flying. As if her heart had taken flight and had the power to soar. Toward him.

There seemed to be a lump in her throat the size of…well, the size of wonder. Most of her life, she'd been careful not to react to anything impulsively. It's not as if she could ever completely forget that she'd been a throwaway kid, an abandoned child. She'd always felt that she had to carefully earn other people's regard.

And she had. Winona had long learned to value herself. She knew she was an especially good cop and did a great job with the kids. She knew that she was respected, well liked in the community—and that she'd earned respect. But she hadn't specifically realized that she had Justin's trust and regard in that way.

Someone who she valued.

Someone who she loved—even if she'd been scared witless of allowing that four-letter word to surface in her heart before now.

It mattered. It mattered like she couldn't remember anything, ever, mattering this much before. And when she launched herself into Justin's arms, he responded with a *whoomph*. Possibly he wasn't anticipating a rib-crunching hug at that instant. Possibly he wasn't expecting a hard-ball pitch of a human female from across the room. Possibly he wasn't prepared for the trembling, hard smash of her lips against his.

But it couldn't have taken him three seconds—maybe less—to figure it all out. Before she'd realized how impulsively she'd reacted, his arms had balanced her—against him—and they were both glued in a lip-lock. The fire shimmered. Shadows whispered on the walls. The night seemed to surround them in a special, private silence.

He kissed her, then kissed her again and again, as if years had gone by since the last time. As if he'd only barely survived since those last kisses. As if the taste of her were all he needed to sustain life.

But it wasn't all she needed. Before, she'd thought it was a fluke, the incomprehensible wildness she felt with Justin. The letting-go. The freeing. The need trammeling up and down her nerves like a clattering train, gaining momentum with every motion. Her hands touched, scraped, caressed, clenched. She tilted her head, taking in his last kiss, then leaned into him to give one of her own.

She had been wearing jeans and a chambray shirt, but not for long. She pushed at his long T-shirt in a frenzy, seeking skin, more playground to explore and touch. After his shirt skimmed over his head, Justin seemed to be slower than molasses, as he unbuttoned her blouse, one button at a time, his lips tracking the path from the hollow of her throat to the crest above her breasts, down to the shadow between. And then his hands were inside, his big warm fingers splayed to caress the span of her waist as he pushed the shirt out of his way. His mouth ducked again, this time to the rim of her bra.

Her breath sucked in, like a lost wave, her lungs scrabbling for oxygen that couldn't seem to be found. She saw his eyes opening, then closing, his face aiming toward her for another kiss, this time on her lips again, this time taking her tongue and her teeth in a kiss that started out sweet and ended up wicked.

By the time he'd pushed the shirt off her shoulders, he'd kissed her shoulders awake as if they were erogenous zones in themselves, and then her shirt snagged at the wrists because of the tight wrist buttons. He smiled—clearly liking that her hands were trapped. Within a millisecond he'd found the catch for her bra, and her breasts tumbled into his hands, her heartbeat tumbling just as fast, just as much in his power, and he took advantage by bending down and skimming her tight, vulnerable nipple with the edge of his teeth.

She'd invited this explosion. She wanted it. But when he

surged back up for another wicked kiss—the bad kind, the scary kind, the kind that took her tongue and her breath and tasted all her secrets—she was quivering like a leaf in a wild spring storm. Justin sensed it, lifted his head, studied her face with liquid dark eyes.

"There's nothing we're ever doing, Win, that you don't want."

"I want this. I want you."

But now he hesitated as if he meant it. "I need you to be sure you want this. Yeah, I'll stop if you say, but I'm really, really gonna be unhappy if we go any further and you *don't* want this. It's all right. Whatever you want is all right, but I don't think you came here believing we were going to do anything like this."

"Maybe I didn't expect it. But I know exactly what I want. And it's you." He didn't get it. Didn't get how much his trust meant to her; his respect. How much something he'd so freely given her, without even having to think, had turned an emotional corner in her heart that simply would never turn back again. She framed his face, kissed him again, this time softer, this time with the "please" buried inside it.

"Well, that's it," he said hoarsely. "You're in trouble now."

"Oh? Is that a promise or a warning?"

"A promise," he said thickly. He pulled off the rest of her shirt. "And I always keep my promises, Win."

A thrill whispered up her spine, an excitement that both embarrassed and unnerved her. The thing was, she believed him. And suddenly she wasn't so sure of the situation or him—or of herself. He left the lights on, the wood fire blazing, but he was suddenly kissing her in a way that made her walk backward, propelling her out into the dark hall.

"Where are we going?"

"I think making love with you by the fire'd be outstanding—another time. On the pool table might be another terrific idea. Another time. But the first time, I want you on a big, hard mattress.''

"Um…"

"Cat got your tongue, Winona?"

He was unnerving her, and he knew it. Liked it. She wasn't afraid of anything. Never had been. She'd faced down strung-out kids and brutalizing adults and even, as a child, stood up every time she was afraid—partly because there'd never been any other choice; she'd only had herself to depend on and she'd learned courage from doing just that. But somehow, right then, she was afraid of him.

Not that he'd hurt her.

Never that.

This fear was a curious thing, elemental, sharp. Thrills and adrenaline kept scissoring up her nerves, electrifying her hormones, charging heat through her whole body. She wanted to dive off this cliff. She wanted to soar without a parachute. She wanted this high-speed chase.

She wanted him.

She was just scared. Of something she couldn't name, wasn't sure of. But when she kissed him, the fear ebbed back. And when she kissed him hard, mindlessly, putting her whole self into it, the fear became something so much fun that she never wanted it to go away.

Her shoulder grazed the stucco wall in the hall. Then a doorjamb. There was no way to recognize anything in his bedroom—not just because she'd never been in there, but because he didn't seem to remember to turn on a light. She had a sense of a long narrow room, lots of space, a chill from a window cracked open. She caught scents—sandalwood and leather. She caught sights because of certain objects shining in the darkness—his metal four-poster bed, a mirror over the bureau reflecting the star-spangled night, his shadow and hers moving past it.

The room was part of him. His. But the textures spinning spells around her were his whiskery cheek, his smooth naked shoulders, the liquid heat pouring off his skin, the silk of his mouth and more of those deep, dark, wicked kisses.

He opened a bedside drawer in the dark, took something out, slammed the drawer. "I'd love your babies, Win. I'd love to make half a dozen with you. But this night, I don't want anyone in this bed—any thought on your mind—but how much trouble you're in. And what I want to do to you."

"What *do* you want to do to me?" she asked weakly.

"Love you. Like I've wanted to love you for a long, long time."

She felt a keening inside. A caving in. Maybe he didn't mean it. A grown-up woman should know better than to believe a man's words of passion...but she did believe him. She felt the truth in his eyes, felt the emotion in his touch and his voice. And that was the last coherent thought she had.

The rest of their clothes peeled off, pushed off. Jeans, socks. Cold air rushed on her bare skin, raising gooseflesh, but then his tongue and mouth covered that gooseflesh, searing kisses everywhere, anywhere. Her elbow, her ribs, the insides of her thighs...oh my, no one had ever kissed the insides of her thighs.

It was payback time. She rolled on top of him, letting him know who was in charge now. In response, she heard his throaty laughter in the darkness, more whispered love words, the hint of more wicked promises glinting in those eyes. He was delighted with her. That's what he'd have her believe. That he cherished, exulted in her letting loose and losing control.

Her being abandoned.

With him.

Finally they were both completely naked. He pulled her hands over her head, stretching them, so that the feeling of length to length was exquisitely intimate, breast to chest, belly to belly, her pelvis rocking against his aching hardness. The thrill wasn't so much fun now. Need started biting at her heels, want gnawing at the lonesome, empty place inside her. "Justin. Come to me," she said urgently.

"I don't want you to forget this."

"I couldn't forget this in a hundred million years."

"I don't want you to wake up tomorrow and think, aw hell, I'm not sure this was such a good idea."

"There's no way I'll regret this. I promise."

"I want this right for you, Winona. I mean it. We can make it right. The two of us—we can make anything right. I know you're not used to the idea of us being together—"

Holy horsefeathers...and they said women talked. She swiveled around and then bent down, thinking that words alone seemed to be completely failing to communicate to him, so she simply had to try another way. She stroked him, then cupped, then leaned even closer. Her caress was tentative because she knew perfectly well this wasn't her personal preference and she wasn't comfortable with it. She understood men liked it; it just wasn't the sort of thing that personally sizzled her toenails. But with Justin...

With Justin, none of the old rules seemed to apply. Different things were true with him, because she didn't seem to be herself. This wasn't just about herself. It was about love. And giving. And the more she tasted, and stroked, and learned him, the more inspired she became by his body's intense and volatile response to her. She heard him groan. Then she heard him growl. She gestured with a hand, trying to say, this was her party and she'd do what she wanted to...but, of course, it was dark, and he likely couldn't see the gesture.

When she failed to respond to his verbal entreaties, though, she suddenly found herself lifted in midair and smooshed into that nice, big, hard mattress again. She vaguely remembered thinking the room was cool before. Now she wondered if his furnace wasn't disastrously malfunctioning. Heaven knew there was a blazing conflagration in his eyes.

"Did you want this over before we even got started?" he demanded.

"Well, no. But I was having a good time. And since I'm the guest, I think you should do the polite thing and let me do what I want."

"How about if I let you do what you want for the next ten years, but I get my way tonight?"

"Hmm. Well, on the surface, that sounds like a pretty good deal...but the more I'm with you, Justin, the more I'm getting the impression that possibly I could get my way all the time."

"Oh, all right," he agreed. And kissed her. Then took her. She couldn't have been more ready for him, yet she was still snug, the fit still tight, and he speared slowly inside that soft, private nest, easing in until his shaft was completely inside her. Colors of sensation washed behind her closed eyes. Sparks of fire seemed to ignite along her nerve endings.

"Justin..." The teasing was gone from her voice. Her belly was filled with him now, yet only ached more fiercely, seeking completion.

As he did. He began a rocking cadence that shook the bed, the room, her universe...whether she rode him or he rode her, Winona could neither keep straight nor cared, but this was a galloping song, a rhythmic race as pagan and pure as exhilaration and joy. "I love you, Win. Love you," he whispered, and then tipped her over the edge into oblivion.

In the dark, afterward, it seemed hours before her lungs could remember that complicated task about inhaling and exhaling. She didn't want to breathe normally. She didn't feel normal. She hooked up on an elbow and just looked at her lover in the dark, savoring everything she saw. The lustrous dampness on his skin, so like hers. The dark satisfaction in his eyes, that had to be reflected in hers. His mouth, as swollen from her kisses as hers was from his.

He lay there, wasted, at least until he opened an eye and realized that she was wide-awake and studying him. She felt fingertips grazing her jaw. "Did I tell you how beautiful you are?"

"Yes, you did."

"Did I tell you how sexy?"

"Oh, yes. In fact, you went into a lot of detail."

"Did I tell you that you're the most fabulous lover and the most extraordinary woman in the universe?"

She bent down and kissed the very tip of his nose. "I'm not even going to answer that. But…if that offer to marry you is still open, Doc…my answer is yes."

She slipped into her house at 4:00 a.m., turning the key in the lock with the stealth of a burglar, carefully closing the door and then tiptoeing through the house until she reached the back bedroom/nursery. Angel was sleeping solid, her little rump in the air, wearing the yellow sleeper with feet. A rush of love hit Winona. She edged closer to the borrowed crib, careful not to make any noise, but just wanting to look and love.

"I missed you," she said in her heart. "I missed you so much. But, Angel, you're going to love Justin."

He really seemed to want the baby. After making love to her a second time, he'd talked for a long time. Both of them were grounded in reality. He understood that Angel's future was a hundred percent uncertain. There was no guarantee that Winona would be allowed to foster or adopt her. The search for the mother was still ongoing. Even if the birth mom never showed up, that still didn't mean that Win had first dibs on the baby. Being married would raise her odds, but that's all it would do.

Winona still wanted to wrap that conversation around her heart. Justin must have said it a half-dozen times. "This is between you and me. It's not about the baby." He'd really seemed to mean it. It was only the timing on the marriage that could help Win's chances with keeping Angel—the sooner she was married, the better. "So why not?" he'd asked her. "If you want a fancy wedding and honeymoon, we can make that happen. But if the baby's the first problem, then let's solve the most important thing for you."

"For me, the baby has to come first, Justin—because she's the one at risk, the one who's vulnerable. If I can make her situation more secure, I feel I have to do that."

"I feel the same way. She's an innocent in a precarious situation, and her needs can't wait."

He really did understand. Yet she'd soberly touched his cheek. "But you can't marry me for the baby's sake, Doc. It's nuts."

"I wouldn't marry anyone for a baby's sake. I agree with you. It's nuts. But just because it happens to be *helpful* for you to be married, why fight it? When it's something we both want and both believe is a good thing?"

"But you never wanted to marry me before."

"Win. You obviously don't know me at all. But you will," he said, and kissed her again.

Now, as she bent over the crib, that memory washed over her in a fresh, warm wave...including everything he'd done to her after that. "I'm crazy about him, Angel," she whispered aloud. "And he's coming over tomorrow. We'll see how you feel about him, too, okay?"

"So..." The soft soprano from the doorway had Myrt's acerbic tone. "You're finally home. Did you have a good time?"

Winona must have jumped five feet—a guilty five feet. She hustled toward the door and out into the hallway. "Myrt, I'm terribly sorry to be so late. I never meant to take advantage of you this way—"

"Lord, girl, I swear you just don't listen. I told you I was crazy about babies. And I offered to stay, how many times, a good dozen? Furthermore, it's not like I was really a stranger to you—you know how long I've worked for Justin, even if you and I never had much of a chance to get to know each other very well before now."

"I know, I know...but I just don't want you to think that—" she scrubbed a hand at the back of her neck, embarrassed "—that I..."

"That you slept with my boss? Well, I should probably say that's none of my business, not to worry—but it wouldn't be the truth. When Justin told me the situation with the baby, that you were working so hard and needed some help—I could see how he talked about you, how he looked. So, to be honest, I really wanted a chance at some matchmaking, at least a little bit—"

"He asked me to marry him," Winona confessed.

Myrt's smile beamed brighter than sunshine. "And that's wonderful, girl. But right now, I think you better catch some sleep while you can. We'll talk about schedules and babies a little later."

"Whatever you're having, I want a prescription for it." Later that afternoon, Dr. Harding happened to pass him in the corridor. Justin had been immersed in a conversation and was unaware how the sound of his laughter had echoed down the hallway until she chuckled, going by.

"She is right." Sheikh Ben Rassad—Ben—nodded with a wry half smile. "You are so buoyant today. So vital and full of spirit. It is good to see you wearing this contentment, Justin."

"Just happy today, I guess."

"Uh-huh. Woman happy, I am thinking." It wasn't like Ben to tease, but every once in a while, his sense of humor surfaced with friends.

Justin didn't confirm or deny his pal's guess, but he knew it was true. All day, he'd walked as if there was a sponge in his shoes and light in his eyes. A gruelingly long workday hadn't sogged down his mood even this late in the afternoon. It was as if Winona were with him, sitting in a place in his heart where she could make his pulse soar, just thinking of her.

Last night with her had been everything he'd dreamed of—and more. All these years, he'd never been sure that Winona would ever notice him, that he could win her, that the chemistry would ever fire for her the way he'd always felt it.

Now he knew better. They had enough chemistry to fuel a couple of planets. Big ones.

Damnation, if he wasn't daydreaming of having it all with her. Really. All. Love. A lifetime. The whole kit and kaboodle.

Temporarily, though, he had to concentrate on serious things. He sobered—as did Ben—when they reached Robert Klimt's hospital room. Both quietly entered.

Although Justin wasn't Klimt's physician, he'd been automatically stopping to check and evaluate Klimt's progress ever since the plane crash. The last time he'd seen him before that had been the night of the Texas Cattleman's Club gala. Justin couldn't say that he'd liked the little banty rooster, but it was still another thing to see the man so reduced. Silent. Helpless. He checked Klimt's pulse, touched his skin, automatically read and assessed all the tubes and machines connected to the patient.

"There is no guessing when he'll wake up from this coma?" Ben asked.

"Not really. His main doctor—Busher—is a good man. He also brought in some outside opinions, just to make absolutely sure he wasn't missing something." Because even an unconscious patient could sometimes hear and take in certain things, Justin was careful to voice his answer positively. "Let's just say that the sooner he wakes up, the more optimistic we're all going to feel. And I'm trying to think what else has happened that I need to fill you in on...."

"Well, mostly what I wanted to know was the status of the patients that were part of the plane crash and could have been witnesses, or known something. But in the meantime—is Aaron still in Washington?"

"Yes. I believe Walker finally reached him by telephone

yesterday, so Aaron at least knows about the jewel theft and Riley Monroe's murder. I just wish he'd get home. No one knows about diplomatic channels and problems the way Aaron does. Obviously no one wants to run around accusing or raising suspicion about anyone from Asterland if we can help it. Relations with that country are precarious enough. But the Asterlanders are naturally getting more and more upset that we haven't found a cause for the plane crash.''

Ben stared at the silent Klimt and all the beating, bleeping machines he was hooked up to. ''If he would just wake up…maybe he saw something, knew something. The fire on the plane started so close to where he and the lady Helena were sitting. And two of the jewels were just as close. If anyone knows anything, it *has* to be him.''

Justin nodded. ''All of us feel the same. We really have no proof that the plane crash was related to the theft. To risk an international incident for nothing gives us all the willies. But I suspect that Asterland is going to send someone to investigate on their own if our authorities don't start coming up with answers soon.''

''I would do the same in their shoes.'' Ben shifted on his feet. ''And in the meantime, we're still missing the red diamond. At least, we can eliminate one suspect from the list. It's a cinch Klimt doesn't have it.''

''That's the only thing we're really sure of right now.'' Justin hesitated. ''What concerns me is that others could be in danger. Whoever killed Monroe wasn't just a thief. He was willing to murder. And if the killer was someone on that plane, there are others who could be vulnerable—either because they saw something or knew something. Even if they didn't realize it at the time.''

''You've talked with Lady Helena?''

''I've seen her every day. She's a trooper. But right now I can't begin to guess if she saw anything. She has almost no memory of the crash. I don't mean that she's suffering an amnesiac condition, but that what she went through was extremely traumatic. What emotional and physical energy she has is entirely focused on her injuries and healing. And she still has months of recovery ahead of her. Maybe she could still remember something, but who knows when?''

Ben paused. ''Well, have you had a chance to talk to Winona?''

''Yes. Last night. She didn't even hesitate. She offered to do anything she could.''

''She understands why the Club wants this kept quiet? To protect the work we do?''

''Yeah. And she understands how ticklish it is, communicating between local authorities and feds and safety agencies and diplomats. It's not that she has power, but it's not power we're looking for, and for damn sure, we're not looking to impede anyone's investigation. Only to make sure the innocent are protected in this complicated mess. She'll help advise us.''

''I have always had the impression that she is a good woman. An unusually special woman.'' Ben studied his face with sudden intentness.

Swiftly Justin lifted a wrist to check his watch. ''It's after five. I have to go.''

''You're meeting her.''

''Yeah. And either you quit smiling at me or I'll have to slug you,'' Justin said wryly, as they both exited Klimt's room with a last glance at the Asterland cabinet member.

''I wasn't smiling at the serious situation.''

''God knows, neither was I.''

''But I admit I was smiling at you. One mention of her name, and you are—how do they say it?—bouncing off the walls. A sudden smile on your face that is close to blinding. Oh, how the mighty do fall.''

''Watch it, Sheikh. We have an expression in Texas. You're cruisin' for a bruisin'.''

''We have an expression like that in the Middle East, too. In fact, I think all countries have an expression like that.

We're meeting again on Tuesday night? To determine what to do with the two jewels, whatever new security measures we want and so on?''

"Yes.''

"Okay. In the meantime, try to remember to eat. To sleep. To not sing in the rain. And to climb down from the clouds before you drive.''

"I'm going to remember this conversation when you fall in love. And I'm never going to let you hear the end of it,'' Justin vowed darkly.

"Yeah, yeah.'' Ben smiled, but then he sobered. "Justin...you have not been happy since you came back from Bosnia. Always, there is this dark look at the back of your eyes, the silence. You work, the long hours, but it's like something is running after you, and you cannot catch it, see it, stop it. This woman...it is good to see you coming alive again. I am glad for you. I mean it.''

Justin was smiling when he walked out to the parking lot. But when he climbed in his car and started the Porsche engine, a chill chased up his spine that had no relationship to the howling winter wind.

He couldn't wait to see Winona.

He couldn't have been happier with how last night had gone between them.

He hadn't thought about Bosnia in a long time now, nor had the chronic nightmares troubled him since Winona had become personally involved in his life. But now, suddenly, he felt itchy, edgy. Win was coming to care for him. Just maybe, the sky was the limit between the two of them. It was just that sometimes, he felt like Bosnia was a smudge of dirt on his face that refused to wash off. Nothing seemed to make those memories go away, not completely.

Forget it, he told himself swiftly. Think about her. Nothing else.

So he tried.

Nine

When Winona heard the knock, she swallowed hard, and then hustled to answer the door. It was just before six, so she knew it was Justin. All day she'd been higher than a kite, looking forward to seeing him again...and she still wanted to see him, but the circumstances had sure changed.

She yanked open the door, carrying Angel. The baby was dolled up to go out to dinner, wearing an ultracool pink jumper with an ultracool pink heart sweater and pink booties. She could have won over the heart of a stone; she was that adorable—if she hadn't been screaming at the top of her lungs.

"Darn it, Justin, I'm afraid—" Winona started to say.

"Eh?" He cupped a hand over his ear, as if he needed a megaphone to hear over the symphonic volume.

"I don't think we're going to be able to go out to dinner," she shrieked.

"Yeah, it does look like we'd better come up with plan

B.'' He stepped in, quickly shut the door on the draft and, as soon as he'd peeled off his jacket, waggled his fingers.

"Trust me, you don't want her," Winona assured him.

"Hey, she can cry just as good in my arms as yours, can't she? I take it we're not in a real good mood."

"She's not hungry, not tired, not sick, not anything, so PMS is my best guess. I just didn't expect it to hit before she was six months old."

"Now, don't be criticizing my second-best girl." He kissed Win first—on the tip of the nose—and then swooped the baby in his arms. Startled, Angel stopped the faucet for a second and looked him over. "I'm the handsomest guy you've seen all day, right, darlin'?"

Winona wanted another kiss. One significantly stronger and deeper and more romantic than that peck on the nose. But Angel seemed to be considering what she thought of the heartthrob with the Sam Elliot eyes in the doorway. Then she decided. First there was a heartrending sniff, and then another melodious bloodcurdling cry designed to alert all neighbors in a ten-mile radius that she was Not Happy.

"Okay," Justin said. "Get your coat and the baby's coat. We're bumping this pop stand."

"Justin, we can't take her anywhere like this."

"Well…I do think she's a little young to be blackmailing us into taking her to Disney World, but I'm almost sure we can come up with something that'll win a smile out of Her Highness."

There were circles under his eyes. There were circles under hers. Winona theorized that possibly the baby guessed what they'd been doing the night before, and wanted to make sure they never, ever, had an opportunity to do it again. But she simmered down for the ride in the car, and only let out an occasional squeal—as if to keep in practice—as Justin carried her into his house.

"I just figured it might work better at my house because I knew we didn't have to worry about dinner. Myrt made something, left it in the fridge. Corned beef, I think? I'm not sure, but I know it's something we could put together quickly. And in the meantime, there's a bunch of things I want to talk with you about.''

She wasn't sure how he managed it. Within five minutes, he'd taken her jacket, ordered her shoes off, poured her a glass of merlot, and was leading her through the house. His bossiness wasn't the surprise. It was all he was managing to do while holding Angel at the same time. And the baby had quit crying—as long as she was bouncing along in Justin's arms.

"Really, Win, it doesn't matter to me which house we choose to live in. If you want to stay at your place, that's fine. But I do have a ton of space here. And Myrt's already installed. Not that those details make this house so great—for one thing, as many bedrooms as there are upstairs, maybe they're too far from the master bedroom? We couldn't hear the baby if we set her in a bedroom upstairs? So then I was thinking, maybe this room would make a good nursery....''

He pushed open the door to his downstairs office, which was wainscoted in teak with a burgundy-striped wallpaper above. Background lighting illuminated his expensive computer setup. A couch overlooked glass doors and the view of the water-garden landscaping in his backyard.

"This is all too dark. I figured we'd throw all this junk—''
"Junk?''

"Stuff. All this stuff could go upstairs in one of the spare rooms. We could just rip out the wainscoting and dark wallpaper. Do baby colors—whatever baby colors are. There's a lot of room for a crib and rocker and all. And next door's a bathroom—although right now, that room's too dark, too. I mean, for right now, we could just make these two rooms work easily enough. It's not like Angel's crawling or walking yet. I can hire a couple of strong backs as soon as tomorrow to start moving the heavy furniture around.''

Once back in the kitchen, he tried to put Angel in her baby

carrier. She let out a prompt, furious squeal. He picked her up again.

He talked about safety gates and baby monitors. He talked about turning in his Porsche for a ''grown-up car'' that would more easily accommodate a baby car seat and groceries. When the telephone suddenly rang, he again tried to put down Angel. Again she squealed. Again he picked her back up again, and answered the phone call while carrying her around.

He found the bread, scooped the lettuce from the refrigerator, knifed on fancy mustard and made corned beef sandwiches on rye, holding Angel the whole time. He looked at the baby once, as if debating whether it was worth even trying to eat without her on his shoulder, and then just ate one-handed.

Before dinner was over, Winona was in love with him.

All right, all right, she'd realized that she'd fallen before this. But some of those earlier feelings were surely lust. And as extraordinarily powerful—and desired—as that lust was, this was a different kind of love. This was watching Royal's most eligible and supposedly most self-indulged and spoiled bachelor working heart and soul to charm a baby. This was watching a doc who'd put in a ten-hour day—after making love to her all night—never lose patience with a fractious little one. This was watching Justin be a father. This was seeing his patience and gentleness and giving nature without him having a clue how much he was revealing.

''Justin?''

''What?''

''You're making all those marriage and life plans so fast that you're scaring the life out of me. You've thought so many things through already, as if you were really that sure—''

''I am sure, Win. We're going to love being married. I just know it. The faster the better. If we don't get all the details resolved ahead, so what? We'll just do things as we go.''

The baby blew a bubble in his face. That was it for Winona. "If you don't mind my changing the subject from marriage for just a minute. I just wanted to mention…if it's all right with you—the very minute Angel goes to sleep—I'm going to jump your bones."

Smooth as silk, Justin chucked the baby's chin. "Well, that's it. What do I have to bribe you with to get you to bed?"

Winona chuckled, but there was no hurrying Angel into doing anything. The baby had had a super day, but something just seemed to hit her wrong around the dinner hour, and she was nonstop fretful—unless Justin was holding or walking her.

"I have an idea," he announced finally.

"Ideas aren't helping us. We need a miracle," she said wryly.

But it seemed that Justin was capable of coming up with one of those, too. In the cobalt-and-marble bathroom downstairs, he started filling the whirlpool tub. While Winona stripped the baby down in the warm, moist air, he fetched candles from around the house, lit them and chose a CD to play a muted, low bluesy sax—achy, yearny love songs, one after the other.

"See how fast I managed to get your mom naked? And you thought I wasn't very bright, didn't you, Angel?"

It was a romantic setting for lovers, not for a baby's bath. The warm jetted water. The candle scents and quivering lights. The yearning love songs. The darkness and nakedness and Justin's dark, soft eyes looking at her from the far corner of the tub, his bare toes caressing her bare toes.

The baby chortled and giggled, either from the safety of Justin's arms, or hers. Angel seemed to think this party had been arranged just for her—which it had—and the little ham managed to keep both the adults chuckling…yet Winona kept looking at Justin. And yeah, she could feel the desire seeping and building between them. But she also could see him relaxing, just as Angel was. Letting down his hair. Letting go.

Possibly because she'd always had such a hard time letting go herself, she had always recognized how closely Justin held his emotions. In his work, he gave freely. It wasn't as if he were a stingy man with his heart. But what he personally wanted and needed in his own life, he rarely showed the world, including her...especially since he'd come back from Bosnia.

Watching the baby try to grab his nose, hearing Justin's gentle laughter, seeing his natural easiness with the darling, Winona fell in love all over again. Deeply. Painfully. Irrevocably.

She rose from the tub abruptly.

"Did you see that view, Angel?" Justin teased. "Your mom is trying to drive me crazy. And doing an outstanding job of it."

"We can't stay here all night."

"*Why?* She's happy."

"Because she'll turn into a prune, you goose. But keep her in here for a couple more minutes, okay? While I go heat up a bottle and fix a place for her to sleep?"

Naturally she'd brought a diaper bag and a change of clothes for the baby, but several hours before, it really hadn't occurred to her that they might be spending the night. Now, wrapped in a towel, she prowled the downstairs, spotting a half-dozen places where she could set up a secure sleeping arrangement for Angel, just trying to pick the best. She decided on the couch in Justin's office, where she could push two chairs against the open couch edge to create a secure barrier. Then there was the business of finding the equivalent of a rubber sheet, and a real sheet, and blankets, and then getting the bottle warmed.

By the time she slipped back in the bathroom, Ms. Prune seemed to be out of the water and was on a thick, fat towel next to the tub, chortling her head off while Justin tickled her.

"Sheesh. We were *trying* to settle her down," she scolded.

"She doesn't want to settle down. She likes being naked. You know who I think she takes after?"

"You. All day," Winona murmured.

"I was thinking about you. To think that you've been walking around my house that way all this time and there wasn't a damn thing I could do about it...it boggles the mind."

"Well, I admit, I'd been thinking about boggling something of yours, too, Doc. But it wasn't your mind."

She was up for flirting with Justin indefinitely...but for a second, words failed her. She caught it. The baby's first yawn. Faster than lightning, she whipped a fresh diaper and sleeper on Angel. And then there was another rosebud yawn when she settled the darling in her arms, those soft velvety eyelashes already drooping as Angel latched on to the nipple of the bottle.

She kept thinking sex and babies shouldn't go together.

She kept thinking that maybe she was nuts, because the candlelight and music hadn't turned her on nearly as much as watching Justin discover being a dad.

She kept thinking that they were teasing and flirting like an old married couple who were already comfortable with each other naked, who already knew the things to say to trigger desire.

And she fell quiet as she fed the baby. So quiet that Justin noticed. She felt his gaze on her face as she coaxed the last drops into Angel, who was all set to snuggle down and sleep deeply now—but Winona didn't want her trying to sleep for the night short on food. Finally, she lifted the little one to her shoulder—all dead weight and baby breath and smelling of powder—patting, rubbing, trying to get up that last nasty burp before putting her down...and still she felt Justin's gaze on her face.

"She's out. Really out this time," she whispered finally. "I made a bed for her in the den. I'll be right back."

Once Winona laid the baby down, though, she suddenly realized how long she'd been parading semi-naked in front of Justin. What had seemed natural before now seemed... different. It wasn't the same situation without the baby as a barrier. That had been like playing poker without ever having to ante...playing at being lovers without ever being alone.

Reality, though, was that they'd only been lovers one night...and Winona suddenly felt an attack of nerves. Technically, this was what they'd both wanted, to have the night to themselves, the baby finally asleep. Only she seemed to be suddenly standing in the hall outside the bathroom, clutched up like a ninny. Surely Justin was tired of the water by now? But would it be presumptuous to go into his bedroom? Should she be getting dressed? And then suddenly she heard his voice, as if he sensed her sudden uneasiness.

"Win? C'mere, you."

It was the lazy, easy sound of his voice that made her tiptoe back into the bathroom, and there he was, waiting for her in the tub with those sexy dark eyes. "Yeah, I know," he said gently. "We've been here a hundred hours already. And both of us need some just plain sleep, don't we?"

"Yes—"

"But how about if you just dip in here for one more minute. I'll give you a back rub."

She hurtled back into the tub with splashing speed, making Justin laugh.

"You're not just a little bit of a hedonist, are you?" he teased, but he wasn't teasing as he nestled her between his bent legs and started working his hands on her neck and shoulders. Her eyelashes drooped as if they weighed five pounds each and her head bobbed forward. She groaned and kept on groaning.

And he kept rubbing and caressing and molding any last

tension from her shoulders, but eventually she heard a different note in his voice. A quiet note. "What were you thinking, Win? When you were feeding the baby a few minutes ago, and you suddenly turned so serious?"

She'd been thinking that she finally believed him—that he really did want to marry her. It wasn't a dream. It was real. All his plan-making for the baby tonight was proof. The way he treated Angel was another kind of proof, that he had strong, tender feelings for the baby and was already taking joy in being a father. But it was the two of them where she kept feeling this rain of wonder. They'd known each other so long...but until Angel had so accidentally slipped into her life, she'd had no idea that Justin had feelings for her.

Now she wondered how he'd fooled her for so long.

And how she'd fooled herself.

She closed her eyes, struggling to offer him a kind of honesty that she never had done before. "I was thinking...well, I almost don't remember my mother. But I remember the morning when I woke up and she was gone. I was pretty young—but I knew I was alone. I remember feeling abandoned, feeling that there must be something terribly wrong with me that she'd left as if I were nothing. And as much as I've wanted a child, Justin, I think I was always afraid that I wouldn't be a good mother. That that fatal flaw in me would show up. The thing that made me unlovable. And I worried that I could do that to a child."

She watched his mouth work, as if he wanted to spill a dozen things to her. Instead he hesitated, and then he just listened. "And...?"

"And then I was watching you play with Angel. Be with her. The joy and fascination in your eyes."

"Well, hell. There's nothing surprising there. She could win a tear from a glass eye."

She smiled softly. "I think so, too. That's exactly how I feel with her. The joy. The fascination. No, I don't know what I'm doing. But this huge feeling of love wells up, this bond to her that just seems bigger than I am. And I know I can be a good mom. I just know.''

"Aw, Win, I can't believe you doubted yourself this way.''

"Well, I did. It's hard to explain, but I doubted…that I could let go. I was angry when I was a kid. I think I always believed under the surface that it had to be my fault—something wrong with me—that made my mom take off. And I was afraid that something-wrong-in-me could affect my being a parent.''

"Winona. You'll be the best parent this side of the Atlantic. And this side of the Pacific, too. You already are. Hell. I didn't know you were worried about this.…'' He hesitated. "When you suddenly got so quiet, I thought maybe you'd found out something in the investigation of Angel's mother—and you just hadn't had a chance to tell me.''

"I'm finding out things every day. But nothing that's helped me pin down where Angel came from, at least so far.''

"Then…you're still worried about keeping her?''

"Yeah, I'm worried about that. Badly. And I'm going to keep worrying about that until we know for sure what's going to happen to her. I can't help it. Any more than I can help hoping that Angel ends up mine. Ours.'' She turned in his arms. "But that's not the reason I'm saying yes to you.''

"Yes to…?''

"I never gave you a clear-cut answer, did I? I mean… you've been making marriage and living plans at the speed of sound. And I know we've come together. I know we've both used the *marriage* word. You especially. But I never came out before this and admitted that I'm in love with you, Doc. Really in love. Off the deep end in love—''

She never got a chance to finish the thought before his mouth latched on to hers. The whole evening, she'd been waiting for this. The whole evening, he'd been seducing her with candles and saxophones and his burping techniques and his blowing bubbles on the baby's tummy…and being in that

tub, naked with him, because dark or not, he had to know
darn well where her eyes were straying all this time.

She made a soft sound of longing, of want, that he sipped
in during another slow, lazy, liquid kiss. His warm, slippery
skin rubbed against her warm, slippery skin. His tummy
rubbed her tummy. Breasts snugged against his chest, where
his wiry dark chest hairs glistened and the orbs of his shoulders gleamed dark gold. His long, strong legs slid and rubbed
against her slim, softer limbs. He was inside her before she
could catch a breath, had her legs wrapped around his waist
before she'd had time to consider whether this was even possible.

"We're going to drown," she feared.

"I already am drowning," he said, and dived for another
kiss, taking her tongue. His hands splayed, clasping her
fanny, melding the two of them even closer together. Inside,
she felt that secret, hot pulsing between them. On the outside,
there was nothing but that womb of water, the magic of him,
the stars on the water surface caused from the candlelight,
the stars in her eyes caused from the look in his.

"I have no protection," he remembered suddenly.

"Good," she said.

Again, his mouth tipped in a slow, intimate grin. "If you
think I mind if we make a baby, Win, you must be out of
yours. I hope we have half a dozen. And I'm warning you
now, my plan for the rest of the evening is to love you 'til
the cows come home."

"Good," she said again.

"It'll be two nights without sleep. We'll both be basket
cases tomorrow."

"Good," she said again.

"If you think—"

Holy moly, how the man could talk. She framed his face
with her hands to pull him closer. Then flexed her thighs to
wrap him closer in that way. He didn't talk any more after
that. Neither did she, although, tarnation, they made a hor-

rible mess. Water splashed over the marble sides, onto the floor. Once they sank under and nearly drowned. He rolled with her on top, then maneuvered her right under the pulsing hot jets where the dark, silky water pulsed intimately on both of them, never separating from her for an instant, never losing rhythm, just spinning, spinning....

Spinning a magic spell, she thought helplessly, that she never wanted to wake up from. Somewhere that night, she lost all her inhibitions. The good ones. The important ones. The inhibitions that she'd cultivated so carefully her whole life because she was so absolutely sure that she needed them to survive. With him, everything was different. With him, she felt as abandoned as she'd ever imagined....

But in the most joyful of all ways.

"I love you, Winona Raye," he whispered, just as he hurled them both over the last crest and tipped them into ecstasy.

The next day, as Winona was driving to lunch with Angel propped in the car seat next to her, she suddenly laughed out loud. All morning, memories from the night before had been rolling through her mind, making her buoyant and smiley all over again...but this time, her sense of humor was sparked for another reason.

Last night, she'd finally said yes to him. In fact, Winona suddenly remembered how many times she'd given Justin an opening to set a specific marriage date. Only he hadn't.

For a man who'd been hustling her to the altar faster than the speed of light, it just struck her funny bone that he'd finally gotten what he wanted—and then forgotten to pin down the date.

Quickly Winona pulled into the one spare parking place in front of the Royal Diner, then scooped up Angel and all the baby paraphernalia it took to get the little one through a short lunch. "You know this place, now, don't you, darlin'? And today we're going to meet a friend."

The minute they walked in, she spotted Pamela Miles, sitting in one of the front booths. "Darn it, I didn't mean to be late, Pam. I hope I didn't keep you waiting—"

"Not at all. I've just been here a minute. And what do we have here?"

Winona smiled, watched Pamela make a fuss over Angel—who hammed up for the attention, kicking and bubble-blowing. "This is Angel, and she's the reason I asked to meet with you. But let's get lunch ordered, okay? I'm guessing that you don't have any more spare time than I do."

Sheila, cracking gum, brought her pad over to take their orders. "Hey, Pam, the bruises are starting to fade finally, huh? You look like you're doing way better, sweetie pie."

"I'm fine, except still having a little trouble getting an appetite."

Winona shot the second-grade teacher another, sharper, look. For a moment she'd forgotten that Pamela had hoped to be an exchange teacher in Asterland for the winter term, and had been traveling on the plane that crashed. "You really are feeling okay?" she asked.

"Fine. Honestly, compared to some of the others, I didn't go through anything. Just some bangs and bruises. Although I have to admit that I was really shook up for the first few days after the crash. It was quite an experience. I still can't seem to eat much."

"I take it that your plans to go over there and teach were put on hold?"

"Yes. I'd still love to, but it'll have to be another time. They couldn't hold the job and leave children without a teacher, obviously, and right after the crash, I wasn't sure how fast I could get there and be functioning. It just made the most sense for both sides for me to cancel out. So I've got a little unexpected time off. It won't kill me to relax until next term—but please, Winona, I don't want to waste your lunch hour on just catching up. I know you said you needed to talk to me seriously about something."

"Yes," Winona said, but then she hesitated. The two women knew each other through their respective jobs. Several times, Pamela had asked her to come in and talk to her second graders, and Winona had loved the opportunity. Before that, all Winona had ever heard was that Pamela's mother had quite an unfortunate reputation in town—which was always a complete surprise to anyone first meeting Pam. She was plain, inclined to wearing dowdy Peter Pan collars and demure, concealing styles. She wore her black hair short and simple, and never seemed to bother with much makeup. Her features lit up around children, though, showing off dimples and big blue eyes. She seemed to be a quiet, genuine person in a way that Winona had always liked. She just didn't quite know how to approach this subject, but she had to start somewhere.

"I'm guessing you've heard through the gossip grapevine about Angel. Someone abandoned her on my doorstep a couple weeks ago. I've been trying to track down the mother ever since."

"You bet, I heard. The whole town's charmed at you running around doing your cop thing with a baby in tow."

Winona nodded. "I know you work with the younger kids, rather than be exposed much to teenagers. But I'm really having trouble finding leads to Angel's mom. I don't know for sure that her mother was a teenager—but it has to be someone from town, because if she didn't know who I was, she'd have had no reason to leave the baby with a note to me specifically. So I was hoping—"

"You were hoping I'd know something?"

"Yeah. I figured it was a long shot to ask you—but all the standard routes I've tried have ended up dead ends. Everyone says that kids all ages just naturally talk to you. So I was hoping you might have heard something about a girl in trouble...."

"Well, darn. There is someone." Pamela tapped her fingers on the tabletop. "I'm trying to remember the woman's name. She was at the Texas Cattleman's Club party early this month—someone said she'd lost a baby before Christmas, but at the time, that struck me as odd. You know how it is in Royal. The whole town would have turned out for a funeral, anything to help someone going through a loss like that. Only there was no funeral—'' Pamela suddenly shook her head. ''This is nuts. I really don't know anything. That was just vague gossip I heard at the time, and to tell you the truth, I was only paying attention to one thing at that party—''

''Uh-huh.'' Because Angel started fussing, Winona picked up the baby and plugged in a bottle, although she shot a woman-to-woman grin at Pamela. ''I saw you dancing with Aaron Black, girl.''

Color bloomed on Pamela's cheeks. ''I felt like Cinderella at the ball—and believe me, I'm not into fairy tales. I'm not usually a party person, either. The only reason I went to that gathering was because I was planning on teaching in Asterland, and I thought I'd have a chance to meet more Asterlanders there…but I just don't belong in a group like that.''

Winona sensed the other woman's insecurity and pounced. ''Hey, what's that supposed to mean?''

''Come on. You know Aaron—he looks like a fairy-tale prince. Tall and sophisticated and good-looking…''

''Well, yeah, he's a nice-looking man.'' Winona knew Aaron. Everyone did. His diplomacy work took him overseas so much that he was rarely home except around the holidays, but she remembered seeing him at Justin's shindig. It was just, compared to Justin, no man seemed hot. Not anymore.

''Hmm. I saw you at that party, too, Winona. It's no wonder you didn't pay that much attention to Aaron. You only had your eyes on one guy yourself.''

''Huh? What are you talking about?''

''Come on. I saw you dancing with a bunch of guys. But you still only had eyes for Dr. Webb.''

Winona was so startled at Pamela's observation that she

accidentally dislodged the bottle from the baby's mouth. Was it possible, that others had noticed the chemistry between her and Justin before she'd realized it?

When Angel sputtered, she popped the bottle back in, unconsciously rocking and soothing the baby at the same time...but her mind was really spinning now. She'd always had special feelings for him. She'd also always seemed to notice things about him that others never saw—like that the playboy reputation he'd cultivated was never true, and that there was a whole emotional side to him that he never showed to the world.

Maybe she'd always felt the seeds of love, Winona mused, and maybe he had, too. But still, something had triggered his asking her to marry him in a serious way. And anxiety suddenly threaded a drumbeat in her pulse. Everything had been going so well, but she still hadn't shaken the sensation that something was wrong. Something not right in Justin's life, in his heart, that he hadn't shared with her.

"Okay, I'll quit teasing you," Pamela said. "If you don't want to talk about your doctor hunk, I won't press. And I promise, I'll keep my ear to the ground on anything I might hear about Angel's mother." She motioned to the baby, and hesitated. "You want to keep her, don't you?" she asked softly.

"Yeah." Winona could feel her eyes burning. "I already feel like she's mine. But what matters is that we know what happened. It's the best way to protect the baby's future long-term. The truth. Not just wishful thinking."

"I'm afraid that's true of life, too. Unfortunately." Pamela suddenly pressed a hand on her abdomen. "I'm sorry. I have to go."

Winona saw the gesture. "Are you ill? Do you need some help?"

"No, no, I'm fine. It's just that ever since that darned plane crash, nothing seems to sit well on my stomach. Maybe it's a little post-traumatic stress or some silly nonsense like that.

It's only been a couple of weeks. I figure I'll be patient a little longer before throwing in the towel and seeing a doc. Anyway..." She stood up, pressed Winona's hand and kissed the baby's forehead, before heading for the door.

Angel seemed to finish the bottle at the same time. Winona lifted the baby to her shoulder, patting her, burping her, still smiling a goodbye as Pamela left...but the smile slowly faded from her face. She snuggled the baby close.

She couldn't shake the feeling that there was something troubling Justin that she didn't understand. Before, it hadn't mattered. Before, it hadn't been her business, her right to know or ask or help.

But now it was.

And now her heart was hanging out there, at risk in a way she'd never risked her heart before. For a man who was worth it. But a man she suddenly wasn't sure really needed—or wanted—her.

Ten

When Justin picked up Winona for dinner, he was so close to a shambling mess that he wanted to laugh at himself. He'd never been a nervous type. Couldn't be. In his work, he had to do hours of intricate surgery without hesitation or allowing emotions to fluster his judgment. Yet tonight, his stomach was flip-flopping, his heartbeat galloping like a clumsy colt's, his palms sticky-damp, and the extremely small package in his suit pocket seemed to weigh five tons.

He counted on feeling better when he saw her—only it didn't work out that way.

For a few minutes she stood in the doorway, giving Myrt instructions and talking about the baby. And while she was standing there, she tugged on a coat, which she was definitely going to need, since the January night was frigid, the stars colder than diamonds against a black felt sky. Still, he'd caught a look at her in the black silk and heels. Even when Win dressed up, she never wore show-off clothes, nothing to toot her figure or draw attention to herself. But something had gotten into her. Something dangerous. Something worrisome. He didn't know what to make of it all—the dipping-to-trouble bodice and the smoky thing she'd done to her eyes and the subtly lethal scent she wore.

His blood pressure had been in trouble before he picked her up. Now it was threatening stroke levels.

He was tugging on his tie even before he'd parked and walked her into Claire's. The restaurant was on Main Street, past the bustling new town, past the shopping district, past the old, historic Royalton Hotel. Possibly five crystal snow flakes fell from the sky—no more, just enough to add atmosphere and magic to the night—and they stepped inside.

Although Royal was a wealthy town because of its oil, the town's personality had never been formal. Claire's was the exception. Just inside the door, there was almost an audible hush. The tables were decked with white linen, each centerpieced with a fresh rosebud. No prices showed up on the menus. The carpet was a luxurious wine, the wallpaper some type of velvet flocking in ruby-red. In the far corner, a piano player wearing a tux played muted love songs.

Once he'd taken her coat, Winona half turned to whisper in his ear, "All right. This is scary. I've been here before. You know how it is. The Gerards used Claire's for special celebrations like everyone else does—at least everyone who can afford it. But I always wondered…exactly what happens if someone trips? Or burps?"

In spite of the five-ton weight of the package in his pocket, Justin started relaxing. How could he have forgotten? Win was as natural to be with as his own heartbeat. Even if that dip in her dress was affecting said heartbeat with drumroll enthusiasm. "It's okay," he assured her. "Nothing bad is allowed to happen in here, so you don't have to worry about it."

"Ah. Is that how it works? I always have the feeling that I'm going to get a run in my stocking the minute I walk into this place. Or, more to the point, that I'll be the only woman in Claire's with a noticeable run.''

''Well, that could be. But if that happens, you could take off the stocking and hand it to me to hide—along with anything you're wearing under that slinky black dress.''

''Justin! This dress is not slinky!''

''It sure is. On you.'' Again, he yanked on his tie. ''Maybe we should go straight home. You're not that hungry, are you? I am. But not for food anymore.''

Winona crackled the menu. ''You are a bad, bad man and an even worse influence,'' she said severely, and then smiled like a saint for the waiter.

''I think we want to start out with the most decadent bottle of wine you've got in the cellar,'' Justin said, only to have Win bat her eyes at him.

''You mean those grapes went out and misbehaved? Created a scandal on their own?''

''You bet. You just can't trust those grapes. Some of them grow up just praying for a chance to raise hell....'' And to the waiter, he said, ''Don't mind us. We're out of our minds. And in the meantime—we want the best steaks you've got in the back—and I don't mean the ones you shipped in from Kansas. We want Texas steaks or nothing—and cooked more rare than a politician's promises.''

''Yes, sir.'' The waiter had a hard time not cracking up, but then he was gone.

''Slip off your shoes, Win. You're just with me. We're going to do the gluttony and decadent relaxing thing tonight or die trying. No thinking about work or babies or worries or anything else, okay?''

Her smile was so sweet he was damn near tempted to sing her love songs. In public, yet. She raised a hand, matching his, touching fingertips to fingertips as if there wasn't another soul in the restaurant. How he'd lived without her this long confounded Justin. And that he could help ease her nerves made him feel sky high…although that moment of private peace didn't last, unfortunately.

Her soft smile suddenly seemed to wax still. "Darnit, Justin, I was really hoping to talk to you…but there are two men sitting over at a corner table by the window. They can't be local, because I'd have seen them before, and there's something a little odd about their clothes. The thing is, though, that they keep staring at you…."

Justin didn't glance over his shoulder. He'd already noticed the two men when they'd first been ushered in. "Yeah. Their names are Milo and Garth. Quite a pair, aren't they? They remind me of a poodle and a pug."

"A poodle and a pu…." Again, she glanced at the two men, and then her soft mouth worked as she tried to control a giggle. "Justin, that's terrible!"

"But true, isn't it?" Once the waiter brought the open bottle, Justin motioned him away and poured the pinot noir into her glass.

"Well, I take it you know them? Oh shoot, they're coming this way."

Well, hell. There were only two human beings on the planet Justin really wanted to see tonight—one was the baby, and the other—the only one he really wanted—was Win. But now he was forced to look up. And as Winona had warned, bad news seemed determinedly bearing down on them.

Milo, the tall one, really did resemble a standard poodle. He was ultralean, with fairly broad shoulders but no butt or body and reedlike legs. A head full of springy, wiry curls framed an angular face with small eyes and a long nose. His sidekick, Garth, was a total contrast. Built short and squat, he had a pug's flat nose and ornery expression. When Justin had first noted them eating, Garth had been shoveling in food as if he feared never getting another meal.

Both now approached their table with courteous smiles. "Doctor Webb, it's nice to see you again. We don't want to interrupt your dinner, but when we recognized you across the room, we thought we should say hello.''

"I'm glad you did," Justin lied smoothly, and promptly introduced Win—although there was a limit to manners. There was no way he was asking the two boys to sit down. "Milo and Garth are here from Asterland, Winona—"

Milo turned an extra-watt smile on her. "Yes, we just arrived yesterday.''

"—and they're here to investigate the difficulties with the plane. Hopefully, by pooling American and Asterland resources together, we're going to find some solid answers soon, right, gentlemen?''

"We all hope." Milo bobbed his head. "Since you happen to be here, Dr. Webb, Garth and I have been going over the passenger list. Do you happen to be familiar with a Ms. Pamela Miles and a Ms. Jamie Morris?''

Justin felt Win's gaze leaping to his face. His ankle brushed hers, hoping that she would pick up the message that he wanted to handle this alone. "Yes. Both young women live locally. Although I would certainly hope that you would be studying the entire passenger list, and not just the two individuals who happen to be American.''

"Of course, of course. It was just that, naturally, the Americans are the ones who are the least familiar to us.''

And it would be far handier to find an American to blame for the plane crash than one of their own countrymen—although Justin took care not to voice that thought. "Well, to be truthful, I am in no position to answer any personal questions about either woman. And neither will Ms. Raye. But both Ms. Miles and Ms. Morris have lived in Royal their whole lives, and I believe you'll find there's no problem with them in any way.''

"I'm sure. Thank you for your time." Garth's flat, shiny eyes acknowledged first him, then Winona.

When they'd finally walked out of earshot, back toward

their table, Winona turned to him with a frown. "The little guy gave me the willies, Doc."

Justin shrugged. "I'm not surprised the Asterlanders sent someone to investigate their plane trouble. I don't think there's anything weird about that. But they hit on me for information right after they got here. I had a feeling they thought they could get more from a doctor than the law. Which just struck me as off base, not the normal chain of questioning…but it's not like it matters. We're going to completely forget about them now, okay?"

"Okay."

"How's my baby today?"

"Your baby started out this morning by charming the entire juvenile court. I swear, the only time she ever fusses is when she's alone with me. In a crowd she never fails to live up to her name."

"Myrt's going to be really unhappy to hear that. She was counting on you needing a nanny more during the day, couldn't wait to baby-sit for us tonight…" They both kept up a light chatter over dinner. The waiter served steak with Béarnaise sauce, snow peas and whipped potatoes. When he got around to taking those plates away, he showed back up offering crème brûlée, which was enough to make Win moan.

"Honestly, I can't."

"Sure you can." He motioned to the waiter to bring two servings.

"You don't understand. I have a weakness for certain desserts. I can't give into it or I'll be fat as a tub."

He heard her protests, but when the dessert arrived, all he heard was "Oh, my," followed by more "Oh, my, my, mys."

He said, "I'm not positive, but I'm almost sure that they generally discourage customers from having orgasms in front of the other restaurant clientele."

"Tough. That's their problem." Now that she'd quit being nervous, Win was back to being herself. Full of devilment and fearless—at least fearlessly diving into his dish of crème brûlée. She'd finished her own. "You *did* bring a wheelbarrow to cart me out of here, didn't you?"

"No. But I did happen to bring something else." He pushed a hand in his right pocket, and geezle beezle, realized his dad-blasted fingers were shaking again.

"Justin…" Maybe Win sensed that something momentous was coming, because she suddenly launched into a nonstop talking fest. "Let's talk about some problems, okay? I don't know what might be bothering you, but it occurred to me that one thing could be the house. You know what I mean. Which house we're going to live in? And it doesn't really matter to me, but my place is so small that your house seems to be obviously the best choice."

"Well, your house is too small for the three of us, but that doesn't have to limit us, Win. If you don't like my place, we could either go house shopping or build from scratch."

"Do you really want to do that?"

"I want to do whatever works for you. And the baby."

"Well…I love your house. So unless you actually want to move, I think it's ideal. Although…"

It wasn't going to work. Trying to talk about anything normal. Not while the box in his pocket was burning a hole in his mind. So when she lifted another spoonful of crème brûlée, he slipped the small black box on the table. When she lowered the spoon, she saw it.

Even though she hadn't leveled all of his dessert yet—and was obviously still hungry for it—she dropped the spoon. She dropped her hands, too. Her eyes met his, softer than lake water and more vulnerable than a spring night.

"Can I…open it?" she asked softly.

"You're going to give me a heart attack if you don't. Not that you have to like it, Win. I wanted to give you a surprise, but in the long run, I want you to have something that you really love and want to look at every day. The best jeweler

I know is in Austin. We could fly up there, and he could either make you something specific to—''

Since she was paying no attention to his monologue, he quit talking. By then she'd opened the box. It was just a ring. Not a diamond, because once he'd become part of the Texas Cattleman's Club, he'd become exposed to the value and meaning of certain gems. The sapphire not only matched her eyes, but a sapphire was supposed to be a stone for a woman who valued her individuality, a one-of-a-kind, as she was. And because he couldn't choose a huge gem, because Win was mightily against ostentation, he'd opted for a priceless one. The hue was unusual for a sapphire, not the dark blue of midnight, but the clear, deep blue of her eyes, the limitless blue of…love.

He'd prepared a speech to communicate all that, partly because he wanted to tell her…but also because he was desperate to have something to say so that she couldn't change her mind. But as it happened, he never had a chance to worry about any of that.

She hurled herself at him. Arms raised. Head tilted. She knocked over a spoon, then a saucer, making enough of a clatter to have heads swiveling from all over the restaurant to witness her throwing herself in his arms. He saw her eyes glistening and almost died to realize she was crying.

And then she kissed him.

Or he kissed her. By then, who could tell? The only thing that mattered was meeting her exuberant kiss halfway…and then more than halfway. Lips touched, and all that rough, fast hurling around was suddenly over. The kiss turned soft and silent and secret. Reverent.

The whisper of her taste was a promise. The texture of her lips a vow. God, she won his heart all over again. Every time she came to him, he felt this horrible melting from the inside. A changing. An instinctive understanding that his life could be bigger with her, his heart could be stronger, the whole universe richer—if she just loved him.

And man, he did love her. From the inside, from the outside, to hell with where they were or who was watching. Nothing mattered but telling her how he felt, what he wanted for her, for them. Love shimmered between them like liquid gold that coated both of them in its warmth and power. And yeah, sexual desire loomed between them, too. Hot and wicked and needy. Craving her was good, too. He couldn't wait to get her out of here, get her naked, wearing nothing but the blasted ring...but it was funny. Just kissing her that instant was all he ever wanted, too.

Finally she eased away, both of them out of breath, their gazes still locked tight on each other.

"I'll be damned. I'm getting the craziest feeling you like the ring," he murmured.

"Don't you try to tease me now, Doc. I couldn't handle it."

He dropped the smile instantly. "I love you, Win. No teasing. No nothing. That's always been what this is about. Not the baby, not anything else in our lives. Just love."

"And I love you. Set a date. Any date you want, Justin."

In the middle of the warmest, most important moment of his entire life, Justin suddenly froze.

Two nights later, as Justin drove to the Cattleman's Club, the roads were empty of traffic—and for good reason. Everybody that could be was tucked inside their houses. Sleet poured down in silver sheets; the asphalt was icy-slick and a fierce wind buffeted and blustered around every corner.

Still, when Justin parked and climbed out of the Porsche, he trudged toward the Club's front door as if he didn't give a damn if the sleet soaked him or not. And the truth was, he didn't.

Win was wearing the sapphire engagement ring. And they'd gone home that night to make love until the wee hours. But he'd also jerked awake around four in the morning from a nightmare, and nothing had been the same since. Something was wrong. Bad wrong. With him.

The crazy thing was, everything was *right* for him for the first time in his entire life. He adored Winona. And the woman he loved more than life itself had freely agreed to marry him. Nine hours out of ten, he was over the moon, feeling as if there was nothing he couldn't do or conquer or dream. Except that when it came to setting a date for the marriage, he got a lump of ice in his throat the size of an iceberg.

Guys all over the planet were petrified of commitment—but that wasn't him. Commitment to Win, forever, was exactly what Justin wanted, so this panicked reaction to setting a wedding date made no sense at all. Until he figured it out, though, he was too ashamed and confused to admit to Win that he was having this idiotic problem. Maybe he could hire someone to punch him out? Beat some sense into him? Shake the screw loose from his mind?

"Justin! Good to see you!" Matthew must have been waiting at the door, because he was right there to push it open. But his gregarious welcome changed focus when he saw Justin's face. "Hell, man. What happened to you?"

"Nothing, just running a little late." At a glance, he could see that the others were all inside, except for Aaron. Drinks had been served. Typically, Ben had his hands wrapped around a coffee mug while the others had aimed straight for the more serious blood warmers. The familiar scent of whiskey was in the air, as were the smells of leather, wool and a brisk, wood-burning fire. Walking into the Club had always invoked a comfortable male-bonding sort of feeling. It was created to be a place where a man could let down his hair.

But not tonight. Not for him.

Dakota stepped forward with a grin. "Hey, man, sure looks like someone rode you hard and put you up wet." But like Matthew, when Dakota got a good look at his face, his smile disappeared. "I didn't mean to joke—you all right? You're not sick, are you?"

"No. I'm fine, really. Sorry to be so late. Afraid I just had a few days in a row with some grueling long work hours." That's what he'd told Winona. He was afraid she hadn't bought it. And it didn't appear his friends were buying it, either.

But they had serious issues to contend with tonight, and no one was wasting time on idle chitchat. The first job on their agenda was finding a new hiding place for the emerald and the black harlequin opal. Before the robbery, they'd considered the safe under the historical mission next door to be both symbolic and as secure as any place could be, but obviously they'd been wrong.

Justin fetched a ladder from the back storage room. The others collected a toolbox and the quarter-inch drill and a broom. The job didn't have to take five minutes, but Justin figured with four men there, it would likely take a good hour.

It took a full hour and a half.

"I'll do the drilling," Ben started out by volunteering.

"I can do it." Matthew stepped forward. "I'm used to doing every type of chore on a ranch. This is nothing."

Dakota hunched fists on his hips. "Yeah, well, I think we got a good chance of running into trouble. Drilling a hole in the paneling is easy enough, but behind that is straight adobe brick. If we're not careful, we're going to end up with a hole the size of a crater."

If Justin had been in any mood to laugh that night, his friends would have easily induced his sense of humor. All the guys were so literally fearless. Men who'd step up, without hesitation, without expecting thanks or reward, to save a child or an innocent. Each of them had literally pledged to do exactly that as Texas Cattleman's Club members—and had.

But hell. Get a bunch of guys near a construction project

and naturally the four-letter words flew…along with arguments over the right way to do things.

Justin would normally have contributed his useless two cents. Tonight, though, when the small hole had finally been drilled—and the swearing settled down—he climbed the ladder in the front entrance hall. The Club sign—Leadership, Justice and Peace—was lying on its side on the ground. And all of them suddenly turned quiet.

Each took one last look at the black harlequin opal and the emerald, before the two stones were wrapped in white velvet inside a film canister. The drill had made a hole big enough to put the film canister inside, so after that, there was nothing left to do but rehang the sign.

"It couldn't be more perfect," Matthew said. "I mean, in the long run, obviously we need to find a more secure vault for the stones. But until we know what happened to the red diamond, this is ideal. Symbolic. Beneath the sign that stands for the stones. We did good."

"Now if all the other problems connected to the theft and the plane crash were only half this easy to solve," Dakota said dryly.

They swept, cleaned up, put away the broom and toolbox. Yet all of them ended up back in the front entrance hall. For them the sign had never been a corny symbol, but an echo of the very real vows they'd made to help others when they'd joined the Texas Cattleman's Club. At the moment, they were all frustrated in fulfilling those vows.

"The more we dive into this mess, the less makes sense," Dakota groaned.

"Let's go over what we know," Matthew suggested. "Nothing's surfaced to identify Riley Monroe's killer yet, has it?"

No, it hadn't—and the red diamond was still missing. As yet, the men had no evidence to link the plane crash to the jewel theft—but the jewel thief positively had to be someone on that Asterland plane flight. Klimt, one of the few who might have given them specific answers about what happened on that plane, was still in a coma. Riley Monroe's killer was obviously their jewel thief, but the cops had no leads or even ideas on Monroe's killer yet…and one of the most curious issues in the whole mess was that two stones had been recovered, and not the third. All the Texas Cattleman's Club directly involved with this—except for Aaron—had gone over the plane with a fine-tooth comb. As had the authorities. As had the two investigators, Milo and Garth, sent by the Asterlanders.

"Well, something has to break," Matthew said. "Part of the problem is that none of us copes well with frustration. We're all in the habit of going out and doing something to fix things. Having to wait is partly what's driving us nuts."

Dakota concurred. "I also doubt that there's a gem as notoriously unique on the planet as our red diamond. Which means that it can't surface anywhere without raising news. Even in the blackest of a black market, it'll raise a flurry when it shows up—if we don't find another way to find it first."

"Yes. The red diamond is really the key to solving the rest," Ben said thoughtfully, and then, "Justin?"

Justin swiftly turned toward them. "I agree with all of you. It's just going to take a little more time. None of us have ever accepted failure and we're not about to now."

The others exuberantly agreed, but Ben was still frowning at him. "Something was on your mind. You were really staring at the sign. Did something occur to you?"

"Yeah, it did."

Justin couldn't explain. Not to anyone. But this strange epiphany thing had happened when he'd taken one last look at the precious emerald and opal. Suddenly his heart had started beating like a drum, hollow, anxious, the *thud-thud-thud* of dread. The missing gem was the reason. The red diamond, for all of them, had always been the true talisman symbol of the group's cause. Not because it was the most precious and priceless, but because it represented the leadership and honor that a good man really stood for.

And the drumming in his heart kept thundering like a hollow echo. Memories of Bosnia knifed through his mind. He'd had such a heroic goal when he'd volunteered to go there. He'd wanted to help. To save people. And at the time, he'd been egotistical enough to believe that he was an ideal person to do that—that he was one of the best docs in trauma medicine anywhere.

Only he'd flown into a nightmare. Patient after patient had been suffering severe wounds from bombs and guns and shrapnel. But the conditions were petrifying. Sometimes there were no drugs. Sometimes there was no heat, no electricity—hell, sometimes not even running water. He had the skill; he had the heart, but he had no way to save them. And patient after patient died, until Justin had started to feel a breaking sensation on the inside. Maybe it wasn't his failures that caused the deaths, but it was still failure. It was still unlivable. And when he'd come home, he'd aimed straight for plastic surgery and away from any medicine where patients died.

It made sense to him then.

It made sense to him for a long time.

It had made sense to him until he'd asked Winona to marry him. All these years, he'd prayed that Winona could love him, but now that she'd admitted to those feelings…aw hell. Justin knew exactly why his heart felt hollow. Because it was. Part of him was missing, no different than that damned red diamond was missing. He was afraid of failing her. Afraid of not being the strong, honorable man that she seemed to think he was—the strong, honorable man that Justin was no longer positive he was, either.

Ben's fingers closed on his shoulder. "Something is wrong. Do you want to sit down somewhere? Find a place to talk?"

Matthew picked up on Ben's concern. "Justin, hell, you

looked like you'd been driving yourself ragged when you first walked in. What's wrong? Tell us. What can we do?''

"Nothing," he started to say. He wasn't sure if he felt more relieved—or more worried—that he'd finally figured out why setting the marriage date had been throwing him for six. At least he was finally getting his mind wrapped more clearly around the problem.

Unfortunately, that didn't mean that he had a clue what to do about it.

Startling all of them, a telephone suddenly rang. The Club, of course, was closed. A call this late was likely nothing more than a telemarketer or a wrong number. But Justin took the excuse to hike for the phone, relieved to get away from his friends' searching attention, no matter how well-meaning their concern.

The closest receiver was in the Club office. He reached the phone just as it rang for a fourth time.

"Justin? Oh, thank God I got you. I didn't know where to track you down...." He heard Winona's voice, sounding not at all like her. Win kept her cool in a thousand crises, and always for others. Yet her tone was shrill with panic and fear. "I need you. Right now. Oh God, oh God. Angel isn't breathing right. Something's terribly wrong. I'm afraid to take her to the hospital, afraid to do anything that could make it worse, I—"

No matter how messed up he was, this was easy. Justin didn't have to think. Winona needed him. That was cut-and-dried. "I'll be there in five minutes flat. I promise."

Eleven

Winona had been afraid before, but never like this. Late that afternoon, she'd discovered who Angel's mother was. At the time, she'd thought that nothing could possibly be more important or traumatic than that—but she'd been wrong.

Right now she was carrying the baby and pacing because she was too terrified to do anything else. She'd been busy, coming home from work, getting some dinner on and the baby down for the night, but everything had been basically fine—until Angel suddenly woke, making petrifying choking sounds.

She was afraid to put the baby down. Afraid to keep carrying her. Afraid anything that she did might be wrong—and yeah, of course, as a cop she'd had first aid. Intensive, extensive first aid, for that matter. But what the spit good was that? There was nothing in any manual about the emotional stakes being so screechy high and unbearable when it was *your* baby who was suffering and you were terrified of doing the wrong thing and risking hurting her worse.

Winona heard the front door open. ''Justin? Back here! Hurry!''

She wanted to brace before seeing him. She knew it would hurt. Winona had no idea what was in that damn man's head, but two days ago she'd finally added up two and two. For days, he'd been pushing her to marry him. First, making out like a marriage of convenience would enable her to foster Angel. Then, making out like he wanted a real marriage. Then, not just making out—but showing her—that he loved her in every way a man could love a woman.

But when it came down to setting a date, he'd ducked one too many times now.

She'd thought they'd had something. And no, she'd never bought into that marriage of convenience malarkey. Since when in the history of men and women was a marriage ever convenient? The concept was an oxymoron if ever there was one. But then she'd started to see how much Justin cared. How much he'd hidden. How he'd be as a dad, how he was as a lover, how much love poured out of him when the door was finally opened up.

Only the blasted man had *made* her fall in love with him. Practically forced her into falling hopelessly, helplessly, deeply in love. And *then* to stall out when it came to setting a date?

Man, it bit. In fact, it hurt so much that she'd prowled the floors for two nights in a row. Right now, though, she had no time for hurt or anger. There was only one thing on her mind—the baby.

She sensed his shadow in the nursery doorway, even before he'd said anything. She heard him yanking off his jacket, hurtling it aside. She didn't look at him, because she was too sick-scared, soul-scared, to take her eyes off Angel for even a second, but she started talking. Fast. ''She's been half choking like this for almost twenty minutes now. Maybe I should have taken her right to the hospital, but I didn't understand what was happening—I also didn't want to take her out in the cold or do anything to make her worse. But I can see—anyone can see—something's *wrong*. She's not breathing right—''

''Keep talking. Just keep telling me everything that's been happening to her.''

''I put her down for the night about forty-five minutes ago. All day she was fine. Completely fine. And she dropped off to sleep right away, only it was like she swallowed something somehow, because suddenly I heard her coughing. I ran in from the kitchen. It seemed like she was choking. I grabbed her, picked her up, started thumping her back, thinking that I could help her get something up—''

''And did you see anything come up?'' Justin's voice was calm, quiet, fast.

''No. But it had to. Because she wasn't choking so bad after that. Still, it's like now. You can see how she's struggling to breathe. Her coloring is almost blue—''

''Did you call a pediatrician?''

''No, of course not. I called you. I want you.''

''Win, come on, you know I don't have any specialty with babies—''

''You know trauma medicine like no one else. There's no one I want but you.''

''Damnation, Winona. You don't know what you're asking me.''

That was such a strange thing for him to say that her head shot up. This moment wasn't about her and him. It was about the baby…but somehow all her hurt disappeared at that instant. She didn't know why he'd ducked on setting the marriage date, but love wasn't the problem. She saw the way he looked at her. His dark hair was still gleaming with melted snow, his cheeks rubbed red from the wind, but his eyes were soft and haunted with love, fastened on hers for one long lonesome second—before he returned all his attention to Angel.

He'd already stolen the baby from her arms, already

moved over to the crib, where he had a flat surface to lay Angel down. Gentle fingers were firmly, swiftly, pulling off the baby's clothes, assessing her, studying, murmuring to her.

"What do you mean, I don't know what I'm asking you?" she asked quietly.

"I can't risk anything happening to Angel. Not her. I can't, Winona, dammit. I *mean* it. I don't do trauma medicine anymore."

It was confoundedly bewildering. She heard his words, but they didn't make any sense. He'd already competently, calmly, taken on Angel.

And the minute he'd walked in the door, Winona had felt herself stop panicking. Well, almost. Her head was still screaming, her knees still shaking, her hands slicker than slides. Because she'd never been the kind of person to panic in a crisis, she wasn't prepared to deal with herself when the symptoms hit so hard. For Pete's sake, it was her *job* to handle people in a crisis and she did it darn well.

But this was about a baby.

Her baby.

And it just wasn't the same.

Still, once Justin was there—no matter what the blasted man said—everything eased. Not her worry that Angel was in trouble. But if anyone could save a baby, Justin could. If anyone could help Angel, Justin would find a way to do it. If she trusted anyone in the entire universe—and there weren't many on that list, never had been for Winona—she trusted Justin.

Quieter than a whisper, he said, "Put on the overhead. Bring the black bag over here for me and open it, would you? And then get me a straw from the kitchen. Quick, okay?"

There was no panic in his voice, nothing to make her worry, yet she instinctively understood to put on the spurs. She returned quickly with the items.

"You know what's wrong, don't you?"

"Yeah," he said. "It's the whale."

"Huh?"

"The stuffed animal. The minute I laid her in the crib—there had to be a reason for the symptoms, obviously? So I looked, and I saw the hint of loose stitches on the whale, the little fuzz of stuffing coming out. I'm guessing the baby put some in her mouth. And I'll bet that's where you were patting her—" He motioned to the carpet to her left "—because she spit some out on the carpet there."

"Oh, my God. Do you think she swallowed some? Is that why she's having trouble breathing? And could it be poisonous? Could—"

"Win."

"What?"

"I need you to listen."

She gulped in a breath. "I'm listening."

"I can't make this pretty. There's still some in her throat. That's exactly what's clogging her air passage and why she's having trouble breathing. It has to come out. Winona?"

"What?"

"I love you. And I promise—I *promise,* Win—she'll be okay. But this isn't going to be any fun to look at, so I just want you to go in the other room and sit down."

She wasn't about to go anywhere—although she did take a couple of seconds to grab the whale and hurl it into the trash before coming back to his side. He kept talking, using a low, easy voice to soothe the baby, but she was the one he was communicating to, warning her that he might have to do a tracheotomy, cut the baby's throat, if he wasn't able to suck the debris with a straw. One way or another it had to come out, and now, and the baby wasn't going to like anything about this, but there was nothing else he could do.

It was an odd sensation, under the circumstances, to be more afraid for Justin than for the baby. But she kept watching him, with her eyes—with her heart. And whether it made logical sense or not, she understood that something was at stake for Justin—something more than the baby, something more than he'd known how to tell her.

And he was right. Nothing about the procedures he tried was pretty, but it was only a few minutes later when the baby suddenly choked and gagged and furiously coughed. And then it was done. Justin eased the little one to his shoulder, patting, whispering, soothing, looking at Winona with wet eyes.

"You tell our daughter *never* to scare me like that again," he said.

Winona wanted her arms around Angel, but deliberately let Justin keep holding her. She did the running, changing the sheets, throwing out everything that had been in the crib earlier in case the stuffing could have contaminated anything else. By the time the sheets were clean and the light turned off, it was past midnight; Justin had redressed the baby in a warm sleeper, and Angel was hard-core snoozing. He laid her in the crib, but both felt the same reluctance to leave her. They both stood there, watching.

Fifteen minutes later they were both still standing, weaving-tired, still watching the baby, even though Justin had said three times that there was really no longer any reason to worry.

"And she's sleeping like a log," Winona agreed. "Come on, this is silly. It's time for both of us to lie down ourselves and get some sleep."

"You go. I'll watch for just a little while longer."

"No, you."

"No, you."

At two in the morning, Winona woke up in the rocking chair next to the baby's crib...and immediately saw Justin next to her in the second rocking chair she'd carted in earlier. His neck looked as cramped as hers felt, his face as tired and drawn as hers must look.

Her mouth softly tipped into a smile, looking at him. He loved her. And he loved Angel. Whatever had been wrong with him earlier in the week, Winona knew positively what the truth was now.

His eyelashes shot up, as if sensing that she was awake and studying him. Just as swiftly, he jerked to his feet and immediately bent over the baby, assessing Angel's happy, little breathy snores, before he could relax and plunk back down in the rocker again.

He rubbed a weary hand over his face. "She really is okay, Winona. This is nuts. We both need to get some serious sleep."

"I know," she agreed, but she didn't move any more than he did. In the dark room, she kept seeing shadows and silhouettes, until the thoughts chasing around her mind finally took shape. "With all this trauma going on, I never had a chance to tell you, Justin. There's no reason that you have to marry me anymore."

"What?"

"I found out who Angel's mother is."

He swallowed, then stood up from the rocking chair and simply took her hand. In the dark, silent living room, he wrapped a throw around her shoulders and then hunkered down next to her on the couch. "Okay. Now tell me the whole story."

"She was at the Texas Cattleman's Club ball. One of the guests. Herb Newton's wife, Alicia. Herb was on sabbatical in the Far East. She was pregnant last year, but then about the time the baby was supposed to be born, she told her neighbors and family that the child was stillborn, that she'd lost it. She had a midwife instead of going to the hospital. The midwife backed up what she said. Herb wasn't part of the birth process. She told him the same thing, that the baby had died."

"But I take it that you found out that she lied?"

Winona nodded. "Yes. The midwife took the baby for the first couple of months. The midwife was caught in the middle of the story, wanting to help Alicia, but not knowing what to do. The problem was that Herb was physically abusive. He didn't stop knocking Alicia around during the pregnancy, which made her afraid that he'd hurt the baby as well. In fact, she was positive he'd hurt the baby. So she asked the midwife to put Angel on my doorstep.''

"God." His voice communicated a wealth of emotion. The fingertips brushing back her hair communicated even more. Her pulse bucked. With love and hope. But there were still things she needed to say.

"Alicia was just one of the leads I was tracking down. But when I caught up with her this afternoon, it all came out. It's not going to be simple, Justin, as far as Angel's future."

"Why?"

"Because she's afraid Herb will kill her if he finds out the baby is alive. She doesn't want the child. At all. It's going to be all she can do for a long time to get herself a divorce, get out of that relationship and start a life over again. But if Herb finds out the child is alive, she's also afraid that he'll demand custody—and because he's the blood father, she's afraid that he could both get it and force Alicia to live with him again—either that or risk him hurting the child."

"What a mess," Justin said quietly.

"Yeah. And that's the point—that it can't be solved legally, at least not for a while. If Alicia gets what she wants, she's going to give the child up for adoption, specifically to me. Or to us." She met his eyes. "But the real point is— there's no reason for you to marry me, just to enable me to foster or adopt Angel. We know the child's situation now. It's going to take a while to fight this out in the courts. But no marriage is going to help or hurt my keeping Angel. The real legal problems are between Alicia and her husband."

"Win, I wasn't marrying you for Angel's sake."

"I didn't think you were, either. But you sure ducked out when it came down to setting a marriage date—as if you really weren't that serious. You hurt me, Doc."

The lines in his face all tensed with anxiety. "That was

never what I wanted to happen. Never. And I always wanted to marry you, Win, for years. From the first time I saw you, and you were twelve and kicking every boy in the shins who dared to say 'hi' to you. God. You were so stubborn. So mean. So full of courage—''

''Quit complimenting me, you turkey, and tell me why you hurt me.''

''I didn't want to. I didn't mean to.''

''Justin—that isn't good enough.''

Silence fell between them, raw and tense. He looked away, then down, then straight into her eyes. ''It was about suddenly realizing...that maybe I wasn't the man you thought I was.''

She laid her hand on top of his, her left hand, so he could see the engagement ring shining softly in the shadows. And then she clipped their fingers together, tight, so he had something to hold on to.

''I lost so many patients in Bosnia. In trauma medicine, you lose patients sometimes. That's how it is. Always. A fight, a war, against death. Emergency rooms are messy, imperfect places, where sometimes you only have a split second to make a life-or-death decision. It's impossible. But...Win, I swear that I believed I was good at it.''

She clutched his hand tighter.

''But there was no medicine over there. Sometimes no electricity. No light, no water, no facilities, no drugs. You'd get patients that should have been saved. Men who never had to die. Children in terrible pain. And there was nothing I could do. Nothing.''

If she could have bled for him, she would have. For so long, she'd known there was a reason for that wounded loneliness in his eyes. The emotion that didn't show. The way he fooled people about the kind of man he was. And she'd known he had secrets, because everyone did. But she didn't know it'd break her heart to hear his pain.

''I thought I was a stronger man. But I came home from

Bosnia and I got the shakes at the idea of seeing another patient die. So I switched medical fields. I see pain, but it's almost always something I can do something about. And no one's died on me. I thought the change was a good choice, but on the inside, it's just been sitting in here—'' he thumbed his chest ''—that I let myself down. Let others down. I wasn't the man I wanted to be. The man I thought I once was.''

''Damn you, Doc.'' So much for holding hands. She reached for him. ''You're so stupid. And I love you so much.'' She framed his face, tight, so that she could smack a kiss on him. A hard, mean, possessive kiss, not a sweet one. Yet somehow so much love poured into that kiss that she felt tears bunching in her eyes like salty thunder clouds. ''You're ten times any ordinary man, you cretin. Did you think you could do everything?''

''No. But...I just didn't realize how much the whole thing had weighed on my conscience. Until we started talking marriage, and we made love, and every dream I had about you and me was finally coming together. And then it just came to me, that I hadn't faced it...being a coward.''

''That's how much you know. Now write it down somewhere so you get it straight. I wouldn't love a coward. Not like I love you. Heart and soul. Sinker and clinker.''

She could see in his eyes, in the way he kissed her back, that it was going to be all right. But he still seemed to need to get more out. ''I just wasn't sure...if you knew me. You didn't know I'd had that failure. And I was afraid that maybe I was fooling you. And me. That I couldn't promise you I was the man you needed me to be.''

''You saved our baby tonight, Doc. Where's the failure? You were afraid. But you still stepped up. You're the best doctor I know. But way, way more than that...you're the best man.'' Again she kissed him, but this time softly. Tenderly. Wanting to show him her heart stripped bare. ''I love you, Justin.''

"Aw, Win. I love you back. So much. That's why I had such a hard time getting past this. Because I wanted the right to love you for a lifetime."

"We've been through a trial by fire, haven't we? But from now on...your fears are my fears. Your worries, my worries."

"And your love...my love," he said fiercely, and took her in his arms, offering a kiss flavored with all the love and promises they brought each other.

Epilogue

When Winona heard the telephone ring, she was surrounded by open suitcases. How one short honeymoon could create so many dirty clothes was beyond her—particularly when most of the garments were itsy-bitsy baby-size. Now, though, she vaulted from the laundry room toward the telephone in the kitchen, delighted to abandon the chore. As she reached for the phone, she heard the muffled sounds of splashing and giggling. Justin was giving Angel a bath—and someone was laughing uproariously. It wasn't the baby.

Winona couldn't help chuckling as she pressed the phone to her ear. To her surprise, the caller was Pamela Miles.

"How nice of you to call," Winona said warmly.

"You're probably really busy if you're just back from your wedding trip, and I hate to bother you. I just couldn't stop wondering how everything was going. If you found Angel's mother and what happened—or what's going to happen—to the baby? If things had settled down?"

"The whole world's going great. And we've just been

back for a few hours—the baby couldn't have loved the honeymoon more. In fact, I actually planned to call you tonight, so I'm extra glad you called.''

"You were going to call me?'' Pamela asked in surprise.

Again Winona smiled, this time a secret smile from the inside out. "Yes. Because I owe you—we all owe you—special thanks. You're the one who gave me the clue to finding Angel's birth mother.''

"Oh.'' Pamela's voice sank, as if she feared that she had suddenly stepped in sensitive waters. "Well, I know it has to be a relief to know the truth about who she is. But does that mean you're not going to be able to keep the baby?''

"Just the opposite.'' Winona stretched the phone cord so she could reach the refrigerator. Still talking, she pulled out a bottle and nuked it, knowing Angel would be hungry shortly for her nighttime feeding. "We've barely had a chance to set all the procedures and legalities in motion, and that's going to take quite some time. But right now, the whole situation looks wonderful. Do you remember the lunch we had, and your mentioning the woman who you happened to see at the Texas Cattleman's Club party early in January?''

"I sure do. The one with the scary husband.''

"Exactly that one,'' Winona confirmed. "I tracked her down. Originally my intent was just to find out the truth about the baby. But I've been around abused women before. Got her talking, coaxed her into calling a psychologist friend. I only wish I'd gotten to her sooner. She didn't get out in time—at least technically—because that son of a seadog she married took another swing at her. This time with a bat. And that was enough. Finally. She pressed charges, and because he'd tried to use that bat, we could make an attempted murder charge stick. She's free, and he's going up the river.''

Pamela heaved a sigh. "I'm so glad she's away from that man. Because he had such a good job and they lived so nicely, the family always looked okay on the surface. But I kept hearing gossip. But I was worried for a long time that there was something frightening going on in that household.''

''Yeah. And she's a nice lady. About time she had some decent luck on her side. Anyway—that all happened while Justin and I were on our honeymoon. She contacted us to formally ask Justin and I to adopt Angel. Right now, she has a lot of work to put her life back together. She wants to move, she is absolutely positive that she doesn't want the baby. I have trouble believing that she won't change her mind, but she says she is one hundred percent sure that this is the right thing for Angel as well as for her. And God knows, we both want to adopt our darling.''

''Hoboy. It's so nice to have a story have a happy ending once in a while. That creep. All that money sure didn't make him a nice man. It just gave him the means to hide what he was doing. Um, Winona…?''

Winona heard the implied question in her friend's voice, but she also heard the sounds of more boisterous laughter. She craned her head to see around the corner. Two streakers were running down the hall. She caught a breathtaking glimpse of two bare fannies, one attached to an extraordinarily adorable hunk, and the other teensy, held high in his arms. Both seemed to be headed—dripping wet—toward the master bedroom.

''Winona?'' Pamela repeated.

''I'm here—I'm sorry—I was just distracted for a second.''

''I understand. You're just home from a trip and you're busy, and for heaven's sakes, you two are still really on your honeymoon. I just want to ask you one more very quick question.''

''Sure. No problem.''

''Do you happen to know…'' from the sound on the other end of the phone, Pamela seemed to haul in a giant breath ''…do you happen to know if Aaron is coming back to Royal soon?''

"Aaron Black?"

"Yes. It's none of my business. In any way. But I was just hoping that you might have heard…"

"I'm almost positive that I heard Justin say that Aaron was due back in town within a few days. And that he's going to be here for a while." Winona didn't add that the men needed to get together for Texas Cattleman's Club business. She just kept her voice light, as if Pamela asking about the distinguished diplomat was an ordinary everyday question.

But once she hung up, and aimed down the hall with the warmed-up bottle, she couldn't seem to wipe the grin off her face. Memories of the Texas Cattleman's Club party whispered through her mind. Something about that party had somehow worked as a catalyst for all kinds of events—some of them dark and serious—but some fantastic, extraordinary events had been kindled that night, too. Who'd have thought that a shy, gentle schoolteacher like Pamela would end up dancing with the sophisticated Aaron Black?

Winona was dying to know why Pamela was asking questions about Aaron Black all these weeks later…but her curiosity disappeared when she stepped into the bedroom. Other events had happened the night of that party. Other extremely unlikely couples had danced together—such as a tough woman cop who'd never planned to get married and never thought she'd belong to anyone. And a doctor with a disgraceful playboy reputation who couldn't possibly fall in love with a woman like her.

Only he had.

Just as she'd fallen in love with him.

Completely. Irrevocably. Hopelessly.

Wonderfully.

She saw the two bodies, naked on the king-size bed, playing and chortling so loudly that she had to tap her foot and harrumph to get their attention. "Just what," she said severely, "is going on here? I leave you two alone for two seconds, and what happens? The bathroom looks like a flood plain. Nobody's dressed. Nobody's dry. And the sheets are all damp now, for Pete's sake.''

Justin's head jerked up, his dark magnetic eyes fastening on her face as if the lovers had been separated for hours instead of only minutes. "Don't blame me for the wet bed." Justin motioned to the fifteen-pound blonde at his side—the one currently suckling on her big toe and drooling at the same time. "It's all her fault. She didn't want to get dressed. She wanted to get her tummy tickled. She made me do it. I'm the innocent one in this story."

"You're blaming a three-month-old baby?"

"Hey, help me out here," Justin told the baby. "Tell your mom the truth. Quick. Before I get in real trouble."

"You're dreaming if you think she can save you." Winona plopped the bottle on the bedside table and dove onto the bed with the two of them. Justin was dead right. He was in trouble—an entire lifetime ahead of delicious, wicked, non-stop trouble. She straddled his waist, bent down and kissed him, good and hard.

Angel chortled when her mom's fingertip accidentally tickled her bare toe, but Winona knew the baby was shortly going to need feeding and putting to bed. The three of them just needed a few more minutes of play first. A half hour from now, however, Dr. Justin Webb was going to have more trouble on his hands than he'd ever dreamed of.

And from the look in his eyes, he couldn't wait.

* * * * *

Watch for the next installment of the

TEXAS CATTLEMAN'S CLUB:
LONE STAR JEWELS

*where the romance brewing between
Aaron Black and Pamela Miles starts to heat
up, and more of the ultrasecret mission
to uncover the missing jewel is revealed in*

WORLD'S MOST ELIGIBLE TEXAN

by Sara Orwig

*Coming to you from Silhouette Desire in
February 2001.*

*And now for a sneak preview of
WORLD'S MOST ELIGIBLE TEXAN,
please turn the page.*

Prologue

———

"**Y**ou're going home to Royal?"

"You heard me right. Can I get the family plane to pick me up?" Aaron Black persisted patiently on the phone, knowing his request was a shock to his brother.

"You're taking a leave of absence," Jeb Black repeated. "I don't believe it, but I'll have the plane there as soon as possible. The diplomat from Spain, my worldly brother, is going to take a vacation in our hometown of Royal, Texas. I'm finding this damned difficult to believe."

"The State Department has cleared it so I can take some time to go home," Aaron said. "Dammit, you take vacations."

"Yeah, with the family and we go to one of those countries you work in. We don't leave Houston to go back and sit around Royal."

"Maybe you should. Royal is nice."

"Yep, if you like cows and mesquite. I'll bet you last two days there and then you'll be calling me to send the plane to get you out of there. What about the embassy while you're gone?''

For the first time that day, Aaron was amused. He smiled in the darkness of his silent Georgetown house. ''The American Embassy in Spain can carry on nicely if the First Secretary is not there for a little while.''

''I'm not sure I'm talking to my brother. Aaron, are you all right?''

''I'm fine. Tell Mary and the boys hi for me. Better yet, give them a big hug. Thanks for sending the plane.''

''Sure. You'll have to admit, though, this isn't like you at all. Aaron—does this have something to do with the Cattleman's Club?''

''Yes, it does,'' Aaron could answer honestly. His brother wasn't a member, but he could have been and he knew that the Club was a facade for members to work together covertly on secret missions to save innocent lives.

''Why didn't you tell me,'' Jeb said, sounding more relaxed. ''Take care of yourself.''

''Thanks, Jeb.'' Aaron replaced the receiver, breaking the connection with his older brother. Aaron stared out the window at the swirling snow. ''No, it isn't like me,'' he whispered to himself. ''Thanks to a tall, black-haired Texas gal, I'm doing things I've never done in my life.'' Mesmerized by the swirling snow and twinkling lights, he remembered early January, the night of the Cattleman's Club gala.

Aaron's pulse accelerated as he recalled the moment he had glanced across the room and seen the willowy, black-haired woman in a simple black dress. When she'd turned, her blue-eyed gaze had met his and, just for an instant, he'd felt something spark inside him. She was laughing at something someone else had said to her. Seeing her wide blue eyes, dimples and irresistible smile, Aaron had a sudden, unreasonable compulsion to meet her. He'd thought he knew almost everyone in Royal, but she was a stranger.

Then Justin Webb had spoken to him and he turned to

shake hands with his physician friend. The next time he'd looked back, the woman was gone from sight. It had taken him twenty more minutes to work his way through the crowd and get introduced. Another two minutes and he had her in his arms, moving on the dance floor. And then later—images taunted him of her in his arms, of the heat of her kisses, her eagerness—memories still fresh enough that his body reacted swiftly to them. Pamela Miles.

He glanced around his quiet living room. Empty house, empty life.

The thought nagged at him. Why did he feel this way so often lately? Except on that night with Pamela Miles. The loneliness, the feeling he was missing something important in life, the hollow feelings he had been experiencing the last few years, had vanished from the first moment he'd looked into her eyes. From that first glance the chemistry between them had been volatile. It had erupted into fiery lovemaking that at the slightest memory could make him break into a sweat. But there was something deeper than physical need. At least there had been for him.

The next morning she had been the one who'd slipped out without a word. When he'd stirred, she was gone. He had tried to shrug off the evening. When had he let a woman tie him in knots? If the lady wanted to end it that way—fine.

But Pamela Miles had a persistent way of staying in his thoughts until he was driven to constant distraction—something so foreign to his life that he decided to see her again.

As he watched snowflakes swirl and melt on the slushy narrow Georgetown street, an emptiness struck him with a chill that was far colder than the snow. Lately he had been too aware of his thirty-seven years and what little he had in his life that was really important. But the night of the Texas ball, that desolation had vanished. Pamela had brought him to life to an extent he wouldn't have guessed possible.

He swore, looking at the phone in his hand as an annoyingly loud recorded message told him his receiver was off the hook.

Aaron stared out the window, no longer seeing swirling snow or the neighboring houses with warm glows spilling from open windows. He was seeing sprawling, mesquite-covered land and a willowy, blue-eyed woman.

"Dammit," he said. "Pamela, I know there was something you felt as much as I did." He shook his head. He was being a world-class sap. The lady wasn't interested. She had made that clear. Maybe so, but he was going home to find out.

The following afternoon, the last day of January, Aaron gripped the wheel of a family car left for him at the airport as he sped down the hard-packed dusty road toward a sprawling ranch in the distance. Mesquite trees bent to the north by prevailing southern winds dotted the land on either side of the road, but all he could think about was Pamela.

He was home and he was going to find his lady.

January 2001
TALL, DARK & WESTERN
#1339 by Anne Marie Winston

February 2001
THE WAY TO A RANCHER'S HEART
#1345 by Peggy Moreland

March 2001
MILLIONAIRE HUSBAND
#1352 by Leanne Banks
Million-Dollar Men

April 2001
GABRIEL'S GIFT
#1357 by Cait London
Freedom Valley

May 2001
THE TEMPTATION OF
RORY MONAHAN
#1363 by Elizabeth Bevarly

June 2001
A LADY FOR LINCOLN CADE
#1369 by BJ James
Men of Belle Terre

MAN OF THE MONTH

For twenty years Silhouette has been giving
you the ultimate in romantic reads. Come join
the celebration as some of your favorite authors
help celebrate our anniversary with the most
sensual, emotional love stories ever!

Available at your favorite retail outlet.

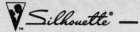

Silhouette®

where love comes alive—online...

eHARLEQUIN.com

shop eHarlequin

- ♥ Find all the new Silhouette releases at everyday great discounts.
- ♥ Try before you buy! Read an excerpt from the latest Silhouette novels.
- ♥ Write an online review and share your thoughts with others.

reading room

- ♥ Read our Internet exclusive daily and weekly online serials, or vote in our interactive novel.
- ♥ Talk to other readers about your favorite novels in our Reading Groups.
- ♥ Take our Choose-a-Book quiz to find the series that matches you!

authors' alcove

- ♥ Find out interesting tidbits and details about your favorite authors' lives, interests and writing habits.
- ♥ Ever dreamed of being an author? Enter our Writing Round Robin. The Winning Chapter will be published online! Or review our writing guidelines for submitting your novel.